THE

MILLS & BOON®

Summer Short
Stories Collection

**Celebrate the summer with Mills & Boon!
Enjoy three classic short stories from
your favourite authors – the perfect little
indulgence for a summer's day!**

M&B and M&B with the Rose Device
are trademarks of the publisher.
Harlequin Mills & Boon Limited,
Eton House, 18-24 Paradise Road, Richmond, Surrey, TW9 1SR

Miss Greenhorn © Diana Palmer 1990

ISBN: 978 0 263 86735 0

077-0709

Harlequin Mills & Boon policy is to use papers that are natural, renewable and recyclable products and made from wood grown in sustainable forests. The logging and manufacturing processes conform to the legal environmental regulations of the country of origin.

Printed and bound in Spain
by Litografia Rosés S.A., Barcelona

Miss Greenhorn

DIANA PALMER

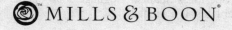

🌀 MILLS & BOON®

Diana Palmer, the *New York Times* bestselling author of more than one hundred novels, is renowned as one of North America's top ten romance writers. When she published her first novel in 1979, fans immediately fell in love with her sensual, charming romances...and this love affair will only heat up with her upcoming books.

A die-hard romantic who married her husband five days after they met, Diana says that she wrote her first book at age thirteen – and has been hooked ever since.

Palmer began her career as a newspaper reporter and columnist – a path she followed for sixteen years. When her first novel was purchased, she retired her press badge and devoted herself to a life filled with romance and penning the page-turners her readers find so hard to put down.

This dynamic woman graduated summa cum laude from Piedmont College in 1995 – at the age of forty-nine! "College was an experience I'll alw ays cherish," she says. "Now I fund a scholarship at my alma mater in my late father's name – he'd laugh to know that it's a science scholarship, when I can barely do math! I also fund a nursing scholarship at the Oglala Lakota College in Kyle, South Dakota, in the name of my mother, who was a nurse."

Palmer is a member of the Native American Rights Fund, the American Museum of Natural History, the National Cattleman's Association, the Planetary Society, the Georgia Sheriff's Association and numerous conservation and charit able organisations. Her hobbies include gardening, knitting, quilting, anthropology, astronomy and music.

Palmer lives in northeast Georgia with her husband, James Kyle, and a menagerie of animals that includes four dogs, three cats, assorted exotic lizards and an emu named George. She loves Spanish-language soap operas and fast cars – her latest is a Jaguar.

Chapter One

It was the second day of the dig, and Christiana Haley was having the time of her life. She'd signed up with Dr. Adamson's Pastfinders team earlier in the year, planning the three-week trip to coincide with her summer vacation from teaching. It was a long way from Jacksonville, Florida, to Tucson, Arizona, but as Christiana had pointed out to her worried older sister, sand was sand.

However, she was learning the hard way that ocean sand and desert sand were amazingly different. She'd forgotten to wear a hat yesterday morning, and he had given her hell. In fact, *he* gave her hell at every possible turn, and had ever since she and the team had registered at his dude ranch. If only Professor Adamson had picked *anywhere* other than the Lang Ranch for the dig. It was pure bad luck that the *Hohokam* ruin the professor was interested in was on property owned by Nathanial Lang, who seemed to hate science, modern people, and Christiana with a passion.

Christy had actually daydreamed about meeting a handsome, charming, eligible cowboy out West when she'd paid the group rate for joining the private archaeological expedition. And what did she get? She got Nathanial Lang, who was neither handsome nor charming even though he was eligible. He'd barely looked at Christy at the Tucson airport and his slate-gray eyes had grown quickly colder. Men had really started noticing her just recently. Her new image gave her a confidence she hadn't had, and it had helped her to overcome her former demeanor—which was shy and awkward and old-fashioned. She had a nice figure anyway, and the new wardrobe really did emphasize it. She was slender and had pale green eyes and long silvery blond hair, a soft mouth and a delicate oval face. She looked very nearly pretty. But Nathanial Lang had stared at her as if she had germs, and he'd made sure to keep his distance from her, even while he was being charming and courteous to the rest of the twelve-member group.

It wasn't her fault that she had two left feet, Christy kept reassuring herself. Just because she'd tripped over her suitcase at the airport and sent its contents flying—and her bra had landed on top of Nathanial Lang's dark head and given him a vague resemblance to a World War I flying ace—well, why should he have been so insulted? Lots of people spilled things. Everyone else had found it simply hilarious. Including, unfortunately, Christy herself.

He hadn't spoken directly to her after that. At supper, a delicious affair served on the ranch's sprawling patio facing a range of mountains that became a shade of pale burgundy in the setting sun, she'd managed to spill a bowl of tomato soup on the lap of her white skirt and while frantically trying to wipe it up with the tablecloth, she'd pulled that off her table—along with most of her supper. It was good luck that she'd been sitting alone. Mr. Lang's mother had been caring and sympathetic. Mr. Lang had fried her with his slate-gray eyes.

The first morning they went out to the dig, she'd tried to get on a horse and had to be helped into the saddle. The horse, sensing her fear of it, helped her right back off again and reached down to bite her.

She'd screamed and accused it of cannibalism, at which point the increasingly irritable Mr. Lang had put her into his Jeep and promptly driven her to the dig site, where he'd deposited her with bridled fury. After a day in the sun, her skin was fried and she'd been no trouble to anybody, preferring a bath and bed to supper.

Somehow, she'd managed to avoid Mr. Lang this morning. Two other members of the party hated horses, so the three of them had begged a ride with the equipment truck driver. It was almost noon, and so far no Mr. Lang. Christy mentally patted herself on the back. She'd avoided him for several hours now; maybe her luck would hold.

Just as the thought occurred, a Jeep climbed over the distant mountain and threw up a cloud of dust as it barreled toward the dig site. A lean man in a creamy Stetson was driving it, and Christy knew just by the set of his head who it was. With a sigh, she laid down the screen box she'd been manipulating for fragments of pottery. It had been too good to last.

He got out of the Jeep and after a few terse words with Professor Adamson, he headed straight for Christy.

"At least you had enough sense to bring the sun hat," he

muttered with a pointed stare at the floppy straw brimmed hat
that shaded her pale skin. "Sunstroke is unpleasant."

"I'm not stupid," she informed him. "I teach school—"

"Yes, I know. Grammar school, isn't it?" he added, insinuating with that thin smile that she wasn't intelligent enough
to teach older students.

She bristled. "Second grade, in fact. I have thirty students
most years."

"Amazing," he murmured, studying her. "They carry
medical insurance, presumably?"

She got to her feet. Too quickly. She tripped over the screen
box and cannoned into a startled Nathanial Lang, tipping him
headfirst into another amateur archaeologist. They collided in
an almost balletic sequence, toppling down the small rise and
into the small trickle of water in the creek.

"I'm sorry, Mr. Lang!" Christy wailed.

He and the other man got to their feet as she made her way
carefully down the small incline, her hand against her mouth.

Nathanial Lang's once-immaculate pale blue pinstriped
shirt was muddy now, along with the deep blue sports coat he'd
worn with it. There was a long trail of mud down one sharply
creased trouser leg, and a smear on his creamy Stetson. He
stared down at Christy with eyes that she couldn't meet.

"Things were so quiet around here before you came, Miss
Haley," he said through his teeth. "And this is only your
second day, isn't it?"

Christy swallowed down her fear. He was tall and very in-
timidating, not at all the hero type she'd been hoping to meet.
"I'm doing my best, Mr. Lang."

"Obviously," he said without inflection.

She reached out to brush off a few spots of dust on his

jacket, but he caught her wrist. His touch, even firm and irritable, was exciting.

"Gosh, Mr. Lang, I'm sorry about that," George, the young
student archaeologist, apologized. George had gone down
the hill with the older man.

"Not your fault," Nathanial said curtly.

"Not Christy's, either," George defended her bravely. He
was tall, thin, blond and wore glasses. He was studious and
shy and had a habit of going scarlet when he was embarrassed—like now. He managed a smile for Christy and
plodded back to his table, where he was sorting and matching
pottery shards.

"A fan of yours, I gather," Nathanial remarked as he brushed
angrily at his Stetson while his slate-gray eyes pinned Christy.

"A friend," she corrected. She shifted. He made her nervous.

"What are you doing out here?" he asked unexpectedly.

Glad for an opportunity to really talk about her work, she
said, "I'm searching for pieces of *Hohokam* pottery. We've
mapped this area and we're doing a pottery search."

"I know that," he said with forced patience. "What are you
doing in Arizona?"

"I had a vacation and I like ruins."

"There's Rome," he pointed out. "They have lots of ruins
over there."

"They've all been dug up," she replied. "I wanted to go
someplace where everything hasn't already been discovered."

"You might try the North Pole." He frowned. "On second
thought, don't do it. There's a theory about the calamity that
would strike if it melted. With your background, who knows?
You might trip over some forgotten thermonuclear device and
blow it up."

She glared at him. Anger gave her delicate features added beauty and color, and her green eyes blazed up. "I can't help having the occasional accident!" she said angrily, wishing she could see him better. He was very tall and his face seemed far away.

He put his spotted Stetson back on his head and cocked it at an angle across his brow. "I'll bet your insurance company has prayer every morning."

"I don't have an insurance company," she managed under her breath.

"Why doesn't that surprise me?" He tipped his hat and started to walk away.

"I'm really sorry about your hat and all," she called after him.

"Lucky for me that it was a little creek instead of an old mine." He stopped and turned, his expression very serious. "That reminds me, there are a few old mines around here, so for God's sake stick to well-traveled areas. If you go down a shaft, you could disappear forever."

She sighed. "Okay. I'll stay where I'm told."

"You'd better," he said firmly and kept walking.

The thought of a mine shaft opening under her kept Christy nervous for the rest of the day. So far all they'd found had been little bits and pieces of pottery, mostly gray. But the fact that it was over a thousand years old made her giddy. Imagine holding something in her hand that a *Hohokam* potter had held in his or hers that many centuries ago! She held one shard up to her nose and drank in its earthy, dark scent with her eyes closed.

They were a very special race, the *Hohokam*. They'd had irrigation and a unique form of peaceful government here in southeastern Arizona about the same time people were hitting each other over the head with battle-axes in Europe. They had a religion which united and uplifted them, a society which was equal for rich and poor alike. They were a poetic people, with a reverent attitude toward the land and each other. From this ancient people, it was said, the *Pima* and the *Papago (Tohono O'odham)* tribes evolved.

"Exciting, isn't it?" George asked, squatting down beside her as she laid the shard back down. "I've read everything I could find about the *Hohokam*. What a pity that their way of life had to vanish."

"At least there are offshoots of it—the *Pima* and the *Papago*," she reminded him. "The *Anasazi* left no trace of themselves as far as we know."

He sighed. "I've dreamed all my life of coming here," he remarked, his eyes lifting to the surrounding sharp, lifeless mountains and the blue sky. "Isn't it clean? Like it might have been a thousand years ago."

"They have pollution alerts in Phoenix these days," she said, "and water and soil pollution are just as big a threat. Toxic waste and radioactive debris and chemical spills..."

George glowered at her. "You're a real thrill to have around."

"Sorry. I have a soapbox. I got hooked on conservation when I was just a little girl. I've never lost the fire. I think the Indians had the right idea—to live in harmony with nature. All we've managed to do is pollute it out of existence. We've destroyed the delicate balance of predator and prey that once sustained the whole planet. Now we're trying to recreate it by synthetic means. I wish we'd left it alone."

"If that had happened, you would be pounding maize to make cornmeal and chewing deerskin to make it soft enough for clothing. I would be hunting buffalo and dodging bullets trying to provide meat for somebody's lodge." He grinned. "In between there would be prairie fires, attack by enemy tribes, rattlesnakes, dust storms, floods and droughts and rabid animals—"

"Stop." She held up her hand. "I agree wholeheartedly that there are two sides to every story." She grinned back. "How about helping me organize these pottery shards?"

"There's something we can agree on," he said.

That night, Christy managed not to do anything remotely clumsy at dinner. She sat out on the patio watching the stars, munching a cookie while Hereford cattle grazed and lowed in a fenced pasture just a few yards from where she sat. The gauzy white Mexican dress she was wearing was cool and comfortable, and her long hair was blowing in the soft wind.

Footfalls behind her made her start. She knew almost without looking who was going to be there when she turned around.

"There's a pool game going on and several people are playing bridge," he said. "I saw a chess match and a checkers tournament. There are books in the library and a television and several new movies to watch."

"Thank you, Mr. Lang, but I find this much more entertaining."

"Waiting for George to show up?" he queried, pausing beside her chair.

"George is playing chess," she informed him.

"And you aren't going to cheer him on?" he asked with cheerful mockery. He lit a cigarette and straddled a chair across from her. He was wearing jeans and boots and a silky blue shirt that clung to the hard muscles of his arms.

She lowered her eyes shyly. "George is just a colleague."

"Not quite what you expected when you signed on?" he

probed. He lifted the cigarette to his lips. "Didn't you come out here looking for adventure and romance? And what did you find? George."

"George is intelligent and kind and very nice to talk to," she faltered. "I like him."

"He's not likely to throw you over his saddle and carry you off into the hills," he pointed out.

"Thank God," she replied. Her fingers clenched the arms of her chair. Her heart was going crazy. Why wouldn't he stop baiting her?

He turned his head and watched her, his eyes missing nothing as they ran down her body to her long, elegant legs peeking out from the skirt of the white dress and to her strappy white sandals. "No taste for excitement, Miss Haley?"

"Being carried off like a sack of flour is hardly my idea of excitement, Mr. Lang."

"Ah. A career woman." He made it sound like a mutated strain of leprosy.

"I'm not a career woman. I have a job that I like and I'm very satisfied with my life and myself."

"How old are you?" he persisted.

"Twenty-five," she said after a minute.

"Not a bad age," he remarked. He blew out a cloud of smoke. "I'm thirty-seven." She didn't say anything and he smiled mockingly. "No comment? No curiosity about my life?"

"What do you do, Mr. Lang, besides run this ranch?" she asked politely and folded her restless hands in her lap.

"I'm a mining engineer. I work for a company near Bisbee. You've heard of the Lavendar Pit, I imagine? It was the biggest mine around in the heyday of mining here in south-eastern Arizona. Of course, now it's little more than a tourist attraction. But we have plenty of other mining interests, and I work for one of them."

"I've heard about the Lavendar Pit, but I haven't seen it yet. I don't know much about Arizona. Do you like your work?"

"Sometimes. I like geology. Rocks fascinate me. I was a rock hound as a kid and as I got older, I found that I liked it enough for a career. I studied it in college for four years, got my degree, worked briefly for an oil company and finally wound up here." He took another draw from his cigarette. "I might have gone to Alaska to work, but my father died and mother couldn't manage the dude ranch alone."

"You…never married?"

He shrugged. "No reason to," he said honestly. "It's a great time to be a man, in a world where women would rather be lovers than wives. All the benefits of marriage, no responsibilities."

"No security, no shared life, no children," she added.

He shifted in his chair. "That's true. Especially, no children. How about you, Miss Haley? Why are you still single yourself?"

"I haven't ever been in love," she said simply, smiling as she glanced his way. "I've had proposals and propositions but I've never cared enough to give my heart." *Or my body*, she could have added.

"I can understand that."

She glanced at him, but she couldn't see him well enough to gauge his expression.

He leaned toward her, his eyes narrowed. "Why did you come out here?"

"I wanted to do something wild just once in my life, if you must know," she replied. "My sister—she's five years older than I am—leads me around like I'm a lost soul. She's so afraid that I'll have a terrible accident and die. Our parents are gone, and that would leave her alone in the world. I can't seem to breathe without Joyce Ann asking if I've got asthma. I haven't been out of Jacksonville in my whole life, so I thought it was time. I escaped on a plane and didn't tell Joyce Ann where I was going. I left her a note and told her I'd call her in a week and tell her where I was."

"I imagine she's worried," he said quietly.

"Probably." She stared at her hands. "I guess it was a cowardly thing to do."

"Why don't you go inside and call her? You don't have to tell her where you are. Just tell her you're all right."

She hesitated, but only for a minute. "I should, shouldn't I?" she asked softly.

"Yes, you should." He got up and reached a lean, very strong hand down to pull her up. For a few seconds, they were almost touching and she had her first really good look at his face.

He had a lean face with a jutting chin and thin lips and high cheekbones. His eyebrows were dark over deep-set eyes and there were little wrinkly lines at the edges of his eyes. His hair was thick and very dark and he combed it all straight back away from his face. He was a hard-looking man, but appearances could be deceptive. He was much more approachable than she'd imagined.

If she was looking, then so was he. His gaze was slow and very thorough, taking in her delicate features like a mop soaking up water. The hand still holding hers contracted with a caressing kind of pressure that made her stomach tighten as if something electric had jumped inside it. She almost gasped at the surge of delicious feeling.

"Don't stay up too late," he said. "You're two hours behind

your time in Jacksonville. It will take a couple more days for you to get used to the difference."

"All right. Thank you, Mr. Lang."

"Most people call me Nate," he said quietly.

"Nate." She liked the way it sounded. He must have liked it, too, because he actually smiled. He dropped her hand and stood back, letting her move around the chair and back to the small guest cabin she occupied. She paused at the corner of the patio and looked back. She made a little farewell gesture with her hand, smiled back self-consciously, and went on her way.

Chapter Two

Joyce Ann was outraged when she found out where Christy was.

"You might at least have asked my advice," the older woman said. "Honestly, Christy, I don't know what's gotten into you lately. The new clothes, the new hairstyle, and going without your..."

"Now, Joyce Ann," Christy soothed, "you said yourself that I was getting into a rut. I'm fine. There are some very handsome men out here," she added, dangling the sentence like bait.

Joyce Ann swallowed it whole. "Men?"

"That's right. Especially one. He's very dashing and romantic, and he's always talking to me." Well, that was true, except that the way he was talking to her wouldn't sound very romantic to her sister.

"Well, he couldn't be much worse than Harry, I guess," came the reply.

Christy didn't like thinking about Harry. He was more of a last resort than a suitor, the kind of man her more staid image attracted. Harry probably wouldn't have cared for the new her. "Harry's been nice to me," she said. "It's just that he wants a mother for his sons more than he wants a wife."

"You aren't desperate enough to marry Harry," Joyce Ann said firmly. "Now tell me about this Arizona man."

"He's sexy and very nice."

"That's different," Joyce Ann said, and laughed. "In that case, I'll forgive you for worrying me to death. How long are you going to stay?"

"Another week or so."

"Good, good. Darling, do let me know how things go. And do, please, wear your—"

"Goodnight, Joyce Ann. I'll keep in touch, I promise!"

She hung up with a long sigh. That was out of the way. Now she could enjoy herself, without having Joyce Ann hang over her shoulder trying to shove men in her path.

The image change was her own idea, though, not her sister's. She was tired of the routine her life had become. She wanted to do something wild, something different. And people had to take chances and do outrageous things once in a while if they didn't want to stagnate. So she'd signed on for this expedition, something she'd always longed to do, she'd bought new clothes unlike anything she'd ever worn before, and she'd changed her appearance. There were a few little minor drawbacks, like walking into people, but in the meantime she was having a ball. Until tonight, she'd actually forgotten Harry and his plans for her.

As she got ready for bed, she thought about Nathanial Lang's attitude toward her. For a man who found her an impossible trial, he'd certainly changed his tune. He'd been almost companionable tonight. She remembered how nervous she'd felt around him at their first meeting, and compared it with the ease of talking to him earlier. It was as if he'd wanted her to be curious about his life, to want to know him as a person. And, she discovered, she honestly did. He wasn't quite the stick-in-the-mud she'd thought he was. He was much more. She went to sleep on that tantalizing thought.

The next morning, she was the first one at the breakfast buffet, to her embarrassment. She'd slept fitfully and her dreams had been confusing and vivid, mostly about the elusive Mr. Lang.

But if she hoped to find a new beginning with him, it was a dream gone awry. He stared right through her as he walked past the buffet and kept going. She stood gaping after his tall figure in the tan suit and cream-colored Stetson, wondering what she'd done to antagonize him now. Probably, she sighed as she put a tiny amount of food on her plate, she'd breathed the wrong way.

"Here, now, Miss Haley, that's not enough to keep a bird alive," Mrs. Lang tut-tutted. The small, dark-eyed woman shook her head. "You'll make me self-conscious about my cooking."

"Your cooking is delicious," Christy protested, embarrassed. "It's just that the, uh, the heat is difficult for me."

"Oh." The white lie produced good results, because Mrs. Lang smiled and lost her worried look. "I forget that you're not used to the desert. But don't you worry, you'll adjust soon enough. Just take it easy, drink plenty of fluids and don't go into the sun without a hat!"

"You can count on me," Christy said with a jaunty smile.

She sat down alone at a table, picking at her food, while the much older Professor Adamson and his wife Nell smiled politely as they passed and went to their own table. The others drifted in one at a time, yawning and looking dragged out. George noticed Christy sitting alone and made a beeline for her.

"What a beautiful morning." He grinned as he sat down with a disgustingly full plate and proceeded to eat every bite. "I never get this hungry back in Wichita. Great food, isn't it? You're not eating," he added with a frown.

"I'm so hot," she said and smiled at him. "I'll get used to the climate in a day or so."

"Lots to do today," he murmured between bites. "Mason's going to use the laptop to match the pottery fragments we've found so far. He spent the night writing a program for it."

"Computers make me nervous," Christy confessed. "We have one at school that we're teaching our second-graders to use, and I'm terrified of it."

"You should see Mr. Lang's," he confided. "He's got one of those mainframe jobs—you know, the kind that cost twenty grand or so. He uses it to keep his cattle records on, and he's got some great graphic software that he uses in his mining work. What a setup!"

"He must be pretty smart," she said.

"Smart doesn't cover it. The man's a wizard, they say. A couple of the gang tried to beat him at chess last night. Talk about ego problems…he could checkmate the best of them in three moves or less."

"I'm glad I don't play chess."

"Well, I wish I didn't," he said with a grin. "Eat up. Time's awasting."

They went out to the dig in the equipment truck again, and

Christy settled down to another day of sifting through sand to find pottery fragments.

She was sitting in the shade of the truck with a soft drink from the cooler at lunchtime when the Jeep roared up. Nathanial Lang climbed out of it, still wearing his suit, and looked around the relaxed camp until he located Christy. He studied her from a distance for one long minute and then went and said something to Professor Adamson before he came to join her.

"You're alone," he remarked, going down on one knee beside her. "Did George die?"

She gaped at him. "I beg your pardon?"

"I'm going into Tucson for some supplies I ordered. Come with me."

Her heart jumped into her throat. "Are you sure you aren't mistaking me for someone else?" she asked, staring into his eyes at point-blank range. "You walked past me as if you hated the very sight of me not five hours ago."

"I did, but that was five hours ago," he said pleasantly. "I've checked you out with the professor. He says you can go."

"I'm not a library book that you can check out...Mr. Lang!"

He'd pulled her up by one hand with apparent ease and she was protesting on the run. He lifted her by the waist, soft drink and all, and put her inside the Jeep, smiling a little as he noticed her attire. Long khaki walking shorts and high beige socks in saddle oxfords, with a lemon cotton shirt that buttoned up and a yellow tank top under that. She'd tied a jaunty yellow-and-white scarf around the band of her hat and she looked very trendy with her long silvery blond hair falling down around her shoulders.

"You look like a teenager," he said, grinning.

She smiled back, shocked by his attention when she'd

given up on ever getting it. "Thank you," she said, feeling and sounding shy.

He let go of her, shut the door, and got in beside her. "Hold on," he instructed as he started the Jeep and put it in gear.

It shot off like a gray bullet, bouncing her from one side to the other so that she had to hold her hat to keep it on her head.

"Doesn't this thing have shocks?" she cried above the roar of the engine.

"Why do we need shocks?" he asked with lifted eyebrows.

She laughed and shook her head. Even a simple thing like going to town took on all the dimensions of an adventure with this man. She held on to the dash with one hand and her hat with the other, drinking in the peace of the desert as they sped along the wide dirt road that led to the paved road to Tucson. Fields of saguaro and creosote, prickly pear cactus and ocotillo, cholla and mesquite stretched to the jagged mountain chains that surrounded Tucson. It was a sight to pull at the heart. So much land, so much history, so much space. She could hardly believe she was really here, sitting beside a man who was as elemental as the country he lived in. Her head turned and she stared at him with pure pleasure in his masculinity, little thrills of delight winding through her body. She'd never felt such a reaction to a man before. But then, she'd never met a man like Nathanial Lang.

He caught that shy scrutiny. It made him feel taller than he was to have such a pretty woman look at him that way. He was glad he'd let his mother talk him into changing his staid bachelor image, and he was especially glad about the improvement when he was with Christy.

"How are you enjoying your stint in the sun?" he asked.

"It's harder work than I expected," she admitted. "I'm stiff and sore from sitting in one place and using muscles I didn't know I had. It's rather boring in a way. But to sit and hold something a thousand years old in my hand," she said with faint awe, "that's worth all the discomfort."

He smiled. "I find the *Hohokam* equally fascinating," he said then. "Did you know that the *Tohono O'odham* are probably descended from the *Hohokam*? And that their basket weaving is so exacting and precise that their baskets can actually hold water?"

"No, I didn't! I'll bet they cost the earth."

"Some of them do, and they're worth every penny. I know an old woman who still practices the craft, out on the *Papago* Reservation. I'll take you out to see her while you're here."

"Oh, would you?!" she exclaimed, all eyes.

"She'll be glad to find someone more interested in her craft than in the price of it." He pulled out onto the paved highway and shot the Jeep smoothly into high gear.

She gave up trying to hold her hat on her head and took it off, clutching it in her lap.

"Not nervous are you?" he taunted gently. "I'd have thought a grammar school teacher would have nerves of steel."

"I need them from time to time," she agreed. She twisted her hat in her hands, enjoying the wind in her hair and the sweet smell of clean air. It was different from the smell of the Atlantic, and not as moist, but it was equally pleasant.

"I suppose you miss the sea," he said, and she started.

"Well…a little," she admitted. "But the desert is fascinating."

"I'm glad you think so." He turned the Jeep on the road that led directly into Tucson. "How do you like Tucson?"

"My first sight of it was staggering," she told him. "I never realized how big and sprawling it was."

"We like a lot of space," he said with a quick smile. "I can't stand to go back East for long. I feel cramped."

"Too many trees, I expect," she replied with a wicked glance.

"That's about it." He sped past fast-food restaurants, modern shopping malls, motels and empty lots. "Did anyone tell you about the coyotes?"

"In the mountains, you mean?" she asked as she looked toward them.

"No. Here in the city. You can hear them howling early in the morning. The tourists get a big kick out of it."

"I wouldn't," she said, shivering.

"Sure you would. You can hear them out at the ranch, can't you?"

"I thought the howling was wolves."

"Coyotes," he corrected. "The Indians used to call them 'song dogs.' There are all sorts of legends about them. One says that they would sometimes stay with a wounded man and guard him until he healed."

"You know a lot about this country, don't you?" she asked.

He smiled. "I was born here. I love it." He turned down a side street and into a parking lot.

Before she could ask where they were, he'd cut off the engine and extricated her from the Jeep.

She almost had to run to keep up with his long strides. In the process of getting into the store, she managed to run into the door and overturn a barrel of hoes and shovels.

With her eyes closed, she didn't have to see the expression she knew would be on Nathanial Lang's face. If she'd had the courage, she'd have stuck her fingers in her ears to keep from hearing him. But no sound came, except a clang and a thud here and there, and hesitantly, she opened one eye.

"No problem," Nathanial murmured dryly. He'd replaced the barrel and its contents and he had her by the arm, an expression on his face that she couldn't decipher.

"I'm so sorry…" she said, flustered.

"Stand over here and look pretty," he told her, leaving her against the fishing tackle counter. "I'll pick up my tags and be back before you miss me."

He did and he was, giving Christy time to gather her shredded nerves and manage some semblance of dignity. Of all the times to do something clumsy, she moaned inwardly, and she'd been doing so good.

"Don't look so worried," Nathanial chided as he came back with a large box over one shoulder. He took her by the arm. "Let's go. How about lunch?"

"I had a soft drink," she began as he hustled her out the door and back into the Jeep.

"No substitute for a good meal," he returned. "How about some *chimichangas* and a taco salad?"

"A chimi-what?"

"*Chimichanga*. It's a…Oh, hell, I'll buy you one and you can see for yourself. They're good."

They were. He took her to a nice restaurant near one of the biggest new malls in town, and she had food she'd never heard of back in northern Florida.

The *chimichanga* was spicy and delicious, beef and beans and cheese and peppers in a soft shell that melted in her mouth. She'd had great fun studying the menu before they ordered.

"What's this?" she asked, pointing to the breakfast entrées.

"*Huevos rancheros*," he translated, "or ranch eggs. It's a little misleading," he said with a smile. "Scrambled eggs and refried beans with salsa. If you eat it, you don't want to sit upwind of any potential victims. It's harsh on the digestive system if you aren't used to it."

She burst out laughing. He was so different than she'd imagined. He was good company and a lot of fun, and best of all, he didn't seem to mind that she couldn't walk five feet without falling over something.

"Like it?" he asked when she'd finished most of the taco salad and was sipping her huge glass of ice water as if it was the last drop on earth.

"Love it!" she enthused. "I could get addicted to this food."

"That's nice to hear." He finished his soft drink and leaned back in his chair, one lean hand toying with his napkin while he studied her at his leisure. "I'm still trying to figure out how a woman who looks like you do manages to stay single."

"I haven't really wanted to get married," she confessed. She smiled at him shyly. She wanted to add that until recently, she'd looked more like a violet than a rose. She'd bought some new clothes and had her hair styled and she'd even taken a brief modeling course to learn how to move and walk. But she couldn't tell Nate that. She didn't want him to think she was a phony. It was just that he wouldn't have looked twice at the woman she'd been. Nobody ever had—except Harry.

His eyes narrowed as he listened to her. So she didn't have marriage in mind. Good. Neither did he. And looking the way she did, there'd been men. He was almost sure of it, despite her old-maid shyness. That could be an act, of course. He'd seen some performances in recent years, despite his lack of looks. He had money. It made him a target for all sorts of women, but especially for the pretty, fortune-hunting variety. God knew, there had been plenty of those around. The dude ranch drew them in droves. He'd always enjoyed the game while it lasted, but he was looking especially forward to playing it with Christy. She was a dish and he wanted her feverishly. Going slow was the hardest thing he'd ever done, but she seemed to want a slow pace, and he didn't want to spoil things.

"Have you always taught school?" he asked.

She nodded. "Ever since I graduated from college. I don't know if you ever really graduate, though," she added on a laugh. "You have to constantly take refresher courses and upgrade your education. I don't mind it. I like learning new things, new techniques. It's quite a challenge to get young minds to enjoy being taught."

"I can imagine."

"You must have studied geology," she said when a short silence fell between them.

He nodded. "I always loved rocks. The feel of them, the history of them, the colors, the forms." He smiled at her over his glass. "I was a rock hound even when I was a kid. As I grew older, mining sort of stood out as a possible profession. It's hard to ignore mines in this part of the country. Tombstone was started as a mining town, and Bisbee with its Lavendar Pit mine was known all over the country for copper mining in its heyday. Even today, seventy percent of all the copper mined in the U.S. comes out of Tucson and Pima County, Arizona. This is the greatest place around for finding profitable minerals, and I don't mean just gold and silver."

"I guess everyone in the world has heard about the Lost Dutchman's Mine in the Superstition Mountains," she agreed.

"Yes. And that's far east of here. But there are rumors that another kind of gold can be found in Colossal Cave, and that's just outside Tucson. It's the biggest dry cave in the country, you know. Outlaws once used it as a hideout, you see," he said, leaning forward to whisper conspiratorially. "And they say the gold's still hidden in there!"

"Wow!" She smiled with excited delight. "Could we go there and look?"

"And here I thought you weren't a mercenary girl," he chided, and the cynicism in his eyes almost gave him away.

"It's the adventure of it, not the prize," she replied, blissfully unaware of the undercurrents. "I'd rather find an old six-shooter or some Apache arrowheads than the gold, if you want the truth."

"I've got a whole collection of Apache arrowheads," he told her. "And if you like, I'll run you over to Cochise Stronghold one day while you're here. Cochise and his band used to camp there. He and his people fought the U.S. Cavalry to a standstill and legend and the historical people say he's buried in an unmarked grave on the site. The Indian agent, Tom Jeffords, who was his friend, was the only white man who was privileged to know the old chief's burial place."

"What is it like there? Desert?" she asked.

"No!" he denied, shaking his head. "It's way back in a canyon with plenty of trees and good water and mountains behind. It's a beautiful spot."

"Imagine that." She sighed, staring at him. "You know, before I came out here, I thought the desert was just a lot of sand stretching to the horizon. But it's not like that at all. It's full of creosote and cholla, ocotillo and prickly pear cactus, and cottonwood and mesquite. And the birds! The red-winged blackbird is so beautiful."

"Not to mention the cactus wren, the roadrunner, and the owls," he agreed, smiling back at her. "Yes, there's life out there. Other kinds, too. Lizards and snakes, coyotes, wolves, deer, game birds—"

"How long have your people lived in Arizona?" she interrupted.

He shrugged. "I don't really know. An ancestor of mine was living in Tombstone around the time of the O.K. Corral, but I don't know when he actually came here. All I know is that he was a Southerner. He came here after the Civil War."

"Someone told me that the city of Tucson once flew the Confederate flag just briefly."

"And it's true. A lot of Southerners settled here in the old days. There's plenty of history here in this part of the state."

"I grew up reading Zane Grey," she recalled wistfully. "I never dreamed I'd actually get to see any of the places he wrote about. But the most exciting part of this trip has been looking at the *Hohokam* ruins."

He nodded. "They fascinate me, too. In 300 B.C., the *Hohokam* farmed here using a 150-mile system of canals. They were an inspiring people."

"Yes, I'm learning that."

He glanced at his watch. "I've got to get back to work. Are you through?"

"Yes, thank you. How can you take off whenever you like?" she asked hesitantly as they got up.

He grinned. "I'm vice president of the mining company. My uncle owns it."

"Oh."

"I'm rich," he said, and a mocking smile touched his lean, dark face. "Haven't you noticed? Most women do."

She flushed and turned away, flustered by the point-blank bluntness. In her haste to move, she backed into the chair he'd pulled out for her, tripped, and went face down across it, plowing into a table full of tourists and their children.

Milk shakes and hamburgers went everywhere. So did the contents of Christy's purse. She sprawled on the floor, feeling unbearably foolish and embarrassed.

"That was my fault," Nate said quietly as he helped her up and proceeded to patch up the incident with a charm and diplomacy that Christy was just beginning to realize was an innate part of his personality. Flinty he might be, but he was a gentleman, and he had a knack for putting people at ease. The tourists were more concerned about Christy than the mess she'd made, and even the restaurant people were understanding and kind.

All that sweetness only made Christy feel worse. She was in tears by the time Nate helped her into the Jeep.

"Now, now," he said gently, mopping up her tears. "I shouldn't have cut at you like that. It was my fault, not yours."

"It was mine," she wailed. "I'm so clumsy…!"

He finished clearing away the tears and tilted her face up to his searching gaze while he surveyed the damage. "Red nose, red eyes, red cheeks," he murmured dryly. His eyes fell to her mouth and lingered there until she felt her toes curling in her shoes. "Red mouth, too," he said, his voice deepening. The hand holding her chin contracted a little. "Red and soft and very, very tempting, little Christy," he said, half under his breath. He lifted his eyes to catch the look in hers, and his gaze held hers until she was breathless from the tense excitement he created.

The interior of the Jeep was quiet with the canvas top on, and they could barely hear the traffic noise outside. The heat was stifling, but neither noticed. His dark eyes lanced into her pale ones and even as he looked at her, he moved closer, looming over her, the spicy scent of his cologne filling her nostrils as his mouth began to move down toward hers.

She felt her nails clench on the expensive fabric of his jacket while her heart tried to climb into her throat. His mouth was very masculine, and it looked hard and ruthless for all its sensuality. She imagined that he knew a lot more about kissing than she did, and the thought of being kissed by Nathanial Lang was far more exciting than she'd ever dreamed. She felt her lips parting for him, waiting, her body in a tense expectation that was suddenly, painfully, shattered by the car that pulled up alongside Nate's Jeep with a noisy roar.

Nate sat up, glaring toward the new arrivals. "Just as well, honey," he said when he noticed Christy's expression. "What we were leading up to wouldn't have been appropriate in a public place. I don't want an audience when I kiss you for the first time."

She choked on her own reply, but he only smiled and started the Jeep.

"Fasten your seat belt," he said easily, and pulled out into the road with apparent ease, his expression as relaxed as if he'd been on a leisurely outing with no excitement at all.

He let Christy out at the dig, and try as she might, she couldn't quite manage to be as blasé and sophisticated about what had happened as he was being.

Fortunately for her, George saw them drive up in the Jeep and came loping toward them, all smiles, with a laptop computer under one arm.

"There you are!" he called to Christy and waved. "I missed you!"

Nate glared toward him. "George, again," he murmured darkly. "Does he have radar, do you suppose?"

"He's lonely," she stammered, surprised by his antagonism for the younger man.

"Is he?" He glanced at her curiously and then shrugged. "Well, to each his own. See you later."

He let her out and pulled away with a shower of dust, without even looking back. In another man, she might have suspected jealousy. But a man like Nathanial Lang wouldn't be jealous of her in a million years, and certainly not of sweet egghead George. She turned with a smile painted on her face to listen to what George was rambling on about. But her mind was still on what had happened in the parking lot of the restaurant, her lips hungry for a kiss she'd wanted so desperately and didn't get.

Nate's behavior was puzzling to her. He seemed genuinely interested in her one minute, and he looked at her with such cynicism the next. She didn't quite know how to take him. She hoped she wasn't letting herself in for a big heartache. Nate Lang appealed to her. She liked to think that the reverse was also true, but she was going to have to watch her step. He was a worldly man with a real sophistication. She couldn't afford to fall too deeply under his spell unless she was certain that he felt the same way she was beginning to. Holiday romances might be the norm here, and she might not be the first Eastern tourist to catch Mr. Lang's sharp eye.

That thought was so depressing that she gave George a beaming smile, and he returned it with interest, thinking it was the lure of his charm finally getting to her.

Chapter Three

Christy had expected Nathanial to ignore her again that night, because he seemed to go from friendly companionship to cold animosity with relative ease where she was concerned. But that evening after supper, he pulled her to one side before George could appropriate her for a chess game in the recreation room.

"Do you dance?" he asked, his level stare disconcerting.

"Why…yes, a little," she stammered.

"There's a bar and grill in town. They have a country-western band and dancing every night. We could sit and drink beer and dance."

"I don't drink," she said, sounding apologetic. Then she held her breath, because he might not want to take her along at all.

"That's all right. You can have ginger ale." He smiled then, and her heart did a dance all its own.

"Then, in that case, I'd like very much to go with you," she said.

"Put on a skirt," he instructed. "Better for dancing."

Was it, she wondered, or did he just like feminine women? But she had to agree when she changed that her full white Spanish dress did a lot more for her than jeans and a loose, short-sleeved sweater had. She brushed her hair out long and wore sandals instead of high heels. When she was ready, she went looking for him. He was wearing dress slacks with a long-sleeved, Western-cut blue-print shirt and a turquoise and silver bola tie, and his feet were decked out in cream-colored boots that matched the Stetson slashed over one dark eyebrow. He looked cocky and arrogant and every inch a sophisticated, mature man. She caught her breath at the thought of spending an evening alone with him and dancing to boot.

"There you are!" George broke in just as she started to speak to Nate. "Why are you dressed up? I thought we were going to play chess."

"I'm going into town with Mr. Lang," she said firmly. "Sorry, George."

The younger man looked unsettled for a moment. He glanced from Christy to Nate Lang, as if it hadn't occurred to him that the other man could possibly be interested in Christy. "Oh, a date," he said hesitantly.

"That's right," Nate said easily. "A date."

"Well, then I, uh, I'll see you later, Christy. Or tomorrow." George smiled nervously before he loped off in the direction of the recreation room.

"He's smitten," Nate told her as he took her arm and propelled her toward his Mercedes.

"He's very nice," she said, defending her colleague. "He's sort of shy and he doesn't mix well. I'm his security blanket."

"You're too much woman to be wasted on a kid who's wet behind the ears," he said.

She waited until he'd put her in the passenger seat and had climbed in beside her to start the car before she answered him. She wasn't quite secure herself, and this man was older than anyone she'd ever dated and very obviously experienced. She didn't quite know how to take his interest in her.

"I'm a little wet behind the ears, myself," she began.

He glanced toward her. "Are you?" he asked, and there was a cynical note in his tone that was lost on her. He grinned. "Fasten your seat belt. Your virtue is safe with me, Miss Greenhorn. For the time being, anyway," he added.

She wondered how to take that, and decided that he was kidding. She laughed softly. "Oh." She fastened the seat belt and tried to look satisfied.

"You're a new experience," he remarked as he pulled the car onto the main highway and sped toward Tucson. "The women I usually attract don't set limits."

"You sound very cynical," she told him.

He shrugged. "I'm a target. I wish I was a little better-looking. Then I might think it was me instead of my bankbook that appealed to the fair sex."

"You must be looking in the wrong kind of mirrors," she said before she thought. She smiled self-consciously at the look he gave her. "Well, you're not exactly repulsive, you know." Her eyes fell to her lap. "You have this way of making people feel safe and at ease with you, and stirring them up all at the same time."

"There's an interesting remark. You can explain it to me a little later on. How do you like the desert at night, little tourist?"

She glanced out the window and sighed as the reddish glow on the horizon threw the jagged mountains into stark relief past the shadowy silhouettes of vegetation across the flat fields. "It's beautiful. Chilly," she added, smiling toward him. "I didn't expect that. The desert is so hot during the day that I thought it would stay that way."

"It doesn't, though. Why do you think cowboys pack blankets in their saddle rolls?" he asked, chuckling. He sped down the highway with absolutely no regard for the posted speed limit, noting her nervous glance at the speedometer.

"Sorry," she muttered. "Back home in Florida, the state patrol will get you for that."

"So will our law enforcement people," he agreed. "But we're pretty far from town here and it's a straight, uncongested highway. I don't take chances, and I can handle the car. In fact, I used to race them when I was in my early twenties."

"Really?" she asked, fascinated.

"Just stock cars," he added. "I did some rodeo, and once or twice I tried my hand at steeplechase. In those days, living dangerously had a special appeal. These days, there's enough excitement in just trying to keep up with taxes and tax shelters, in between prospecting for new finds."

"I don't suppose I've ever done anything really dangerous," she remarked, her pale eyes sparkling with faint humor. "Except maybe riding in that Jeep with you," she added, glancing deliberately at him.

He laughed with pure delight. "You were holding on hard enough, that's for sure. Well, we won't do anything that exciting tonight."

She wanted to tell him that just being with him was exciting, but she didn't quite have the nerve.

The bar and grill was in a nice part of town, and it wasn't a dive at all. It was one of those big, airy places with a distinctly Western atmosphere that catered to city cowboys. It featured a mechanical bull, a dance floor and band, and a light show that was a delight in itself. Nate found them a table facing the band and dance floor and seated her before he went to get them something to drink.

"What do you fancy? Just ginger ale?" he asked politely.

"Just that," she agreed.

He pursed his thin lips and stared down at her speculatively. "Do you like the taste of beer?" he asked with a deep, dark kind of velvet in his voice.

Her breath jerked a little. "Well…not really," she admitted.

"In that case, I think I'll stick to ginger ale, myself," he said and smiled slowly. He left her and went toward the bar.

She sat trying to get her breath back while she watched the people on the dance floor and listened to the music. Shortly after Nate left, a young, good-looking cowboy stopped by her table and smiled at her.

"Hi, pretty girl," he said. "Care to dance?"

"No, thank you," she said, smiling back. "I'm with someone."

"Hell, so am I, but that's okay. We're friendly here." He moved a little closer, and looked as if he didn't mean to take "no" for an answer. "Just one dance, and I'll bring you right back."

She didn't want to dance with him, but it didn't look as if she could find a way out without causing a scene.

Just then, Nate came back with two glasses of ginger ale and moved deliberately between Christy, who was still seated, and the cowboy, who wasn't.

He put the glasses down and straightened to face the cowboy, who looked a little less confident. Talk about body language, Christy thought dazedly, watching. Nate's was emphatic and frankly threatening, especially the way he stood, legs slightly apart, both hands by his sides. He was smiling, but it was not a polite smile. This was a side of Nate that Christy hadn't seen before, and she began to understand that ranching wouldn't be a job for a city cowboy. Neither would mining. Nate had mostly been pleasant and easygoing with her, but there was a toughness in him that she was seeing for the first time.

The young cowboy looked a little nervous now. He could see, as Christy could, that Nate was half a head taller than he was and a good bit more muscular, and had an arrogance and authority that the younger man lacked.

"We came here to dance and have a good time," Nate told the cowboy. "But her idea of a good time and mine are a little different. Now, me, I like a good fight, and I really enjoy making holes in glass. In fact, you're just the right size to make a nice big hole in that plate glass window out front…"

"I see my girl over there," the cowboy said suddenly, making as if to look over Nate's shoulder. "Hi, hon!" he called. "Sorry, but I'd better go now," he told Christy. He tilted the brim of his hat respectfully, looked at Nate and cleared his throat, and made a quick exit.

Christy blew out the breath she'd been holding. "I didn't know what to do," she said as he sat down. Her face was red and she was almost babbling with nerves. "He asked me to dance. He wasn't insulting or anything, but he just wouldn't go away."

"Can't say I blame him," Nate said, smiling gently. "You're a dish."

Her face grew radiant. "I am?" she asked shyly.

That attitude amused him. She was good, he'd give her that. The way she'd refused the cowboy and pretended to be frightened was a nice touch. Not that it worked. He'd seen other women use the same tactic. In fact, he was a veteran. One too many sophisticated Eastern women had come out here pretending to be innocent for his benefit. He was too worldly wise to be taken in, unfortunately for Christy.

"Come here." He stood up and pulled her into his arms, moving her out onto the dance floor to the rhythm of a slow love song. "Relax, honey," he said gently when he felt her slender body tense, going along with the deception to put her at ease.

She bit her lip. "I haven't danced much…"

Sure, he thought cynically. "You'll get the hang of it. Here, put both arms around me. Just like this." He pushed her arms under his and around him and slid his own arms around her shoulders, riveting her body to his so that the only space between them was at the hips. He chuckled at the shiver that went through her, his breath warm and amused at her ear. "Don't you like dancing close? I do." He wondered why she insisted on pretending to be shy and innocent, but perhaps it was part of her act. He didn't care. She was like all the other women who came on to him, this was just a different ploy. It wouldn't matter in the long run. She'd be gone soon, so he was going to enjoy her while he could. She appealed to his senses in a shockingly fierce way. He wanted her as he'd never wanted anyone else.

Christy felt his arms contract and her knees threatened to give way beneath her. Nate smelled spicy and manly and she loved the warmth of his lean body and the hard, heavy beat of his heart at her ear. He was so much taller than she was that her cheek lay against his breastbone. He felt like hard muscle all over and she loved the safety and excitement of his arms. Her eyes closed and she relaxed all at once, letting him take her weight.

He let out a breath himself when he felt her breasts soften against him as she let go. He tugged her a little closer, lifting her into a warmer embrace as he moved her to the music. It had been a long time since he'd felt so exhilarated from a simple dance.

He was no fancy Dan on the floor, but he wasn't bad, and Christy laughed as he whirled her around to the music. She'd been lonely for so long. It was incredible to be here with this man, to feel like a woman, to be free of all the old restraints. This holiday was worth every penny it had cost, and it still would be when she went back home to Florida, back to her old life. She pushed away the thought of leaving Nate, because it stung. She closed her eyes and pressed closer into his hard arms, oblivious to everything except the music and the man.

He felt that tiny movement and his arms tightened protectively. She appealed to everything masculine in him. It was like an avalanche; he was in half over his head already. He couldn't stop what was happening, and he didn't want to, anyway. What harm could there be in another holiday romance?

"Having fun?" he murmured.

"Oh, yes!" She sighed and nuzzled her cheek against his chest, faintly curious about the way he stiffened when she did it.

He stopped in the middle of the dance floor and lifted his head, looking down at her regardless of the amused glances from passing dancers.

"What is it?" she asked.

He wasn't smiling. He looked somber and very adult as he held her eyes. "Nothing," he said after a minute.

He swung her back into the dance, but his behavior had unsettled her. She stumbled and he caught her, the action bringing one of his long legs briefly between both of hers. She clutched at his arms and gasped out loud at the intimate contact.

He stopped dancing again and stared into her soft eyes, holding her shocked gaze while the throng of dancers around them passed by in a blaze of colorful movement.

"Christy," he said huskily.

With fascinated disbelief she watched his dark head bend. He couldn't; he wouldn't! Not here!

But he could, and he did. His thin, hard lips touched hers in a soft, searching kiss while his eyes held hers and the world seemed to spin away.

"You taste sweet," he murmured deeply. His mouth found hers again and this time his arm came up behind her head to force her lips into his. The kiss became swiftly intimate and intense and she moaned with the warm crush of it. "It's all right," he bit off against her lips. "I feel it just that strongly...." The pressure of his mouth increased and she gasped under it.

He lifted his head, leaving the taste of ginger ale and mint on her lips as he looked down at her. His eyes had darkened and his face was totally without expression.

"I want more than a kiss on a dance floor. I'd rather park the car on a ridge and make a little love to you than shuffle around here all night. How about you?" he asked tersely.

She couldn't believe what he was saying, and her face registered that. "I...I..." was all she could get out, when she wanted to tell him that she'd go anywhere, do anything he asked of her. That slow kiss had knocked the resistance right out of her, and he had to know it. His eyes told her that he did, that he knew and understood everything she was feeling, including her faint apprehension.

"I won't rush you," he said. His voice sounded deeper and a little husky. His hands tightened on her upper arms. "Come on, Christy."

He took the decision out of her hands, which was just as well, because she was in no condition to make one. She followed him like a lamb out to the Mercedes, not protesting when he drove quickly and silently out of town and up a winding mountain road to stop eventually by a rock wall overlooking the city.

He cut off the engine and turned to her, his face quiet and somber in the faint light that drifted up from the city streets far below.

"Come here, honey," he said gently. And he reached for her.

She felt the cool mountain breeze drift over her face while he kissed her, savoring the mingled scents of clean air and Nate's spicy cologne as his lips brushed leisurely all over her face. She lay in his arms, across his lap, with his breath sighing out heavily through his nose while his mouth began to possess hers with relentless intent. She tangled her fingers in the thick, cool hair at his nape with more instinct than experience, her nails faintly abrasive.

"I like that," he said under his breath. He lifted his head and studied her rapt face. His lean fingers traced the soft lines of her chin and throat, making her tingle with new sensations. "I'm glad you came to Arizona, Christy."

"So am I." Her pale eyes searched his dark ones in the faint light. "Kiss me, Nate," she whispered unsteadily.

His blood surged in his veins like a tidal wave. His lean

hand lifted her head and he bent, crushing her mouth under his in little, biting kisses that made her gasp, arching her body against his as she gave in to the experienced caresses.

He guided her arms around his neck and his warm hands stroked up and down her back while he deepened the kiss in a way that brought a shocked gasp from her. He could almost feel the surprise in her, as if a kiss had never affected her so strongly. But after a minute, she relaxed and her lips began to respond, shyly, to his.

The response went to his head. He had a pretty good idea that she was feeling a desire for him that she'd never felt for anyone else. Perhaps even sophisticated women were vulnerable once in a while, but he didn't want love from her. He didn't want forever. He only wanted a night. He looked down at her with a deep scowl. She was still and shaken, her eyes enormous in her pale face, looking back at him with a curious kind of expression. He wondered if it would be too soon to make a move on her, and decided that it would. She didn't seem like the kind of woman who made quick decisions about a man. Just as well, he assured himself. He didn't want to start something until she was almost ready to leave for home. It would be easier for both of them if it was a brief affair, quickly over.

She didn't know what he was planning. She saw a dark, intent look in his eyes that thrilled her, because she mistook it for the beginnings of love. She knew that she was falling in love with him. It could have been because no other man had ever paid her any real attention. Well, except for Harry, she thought ruefully. She wondered what he'd say if she told him that there was a widower named Harry with three kids who wanted to marry her? He needed a mother for his sons more than he needed a wife, and he was about as exciting as a worn pair of sneakers. But he was a teacher with a stable income, he had a nice house, and the kids weren't bad. She'd have a comfortable life. Except that she didn't love Harry, and she was beginning to love Nate. Despite the differences between them, his wealth and her lack of it, his Western heritage and her Eastern one, she thought there might be a chance for them. And heaven knew, he did seem to want her desperately, if that expression on his face was any indication of what he was feeling.

Even as she thought it, he was easing her back into her own seat, fastening her seat belt.

"We'd better get back," he said quietly. He started the car and they turned toward the ranch.

He didn't speak as he drove. She was getting to him. Now that he'd had a taste of her, he knew he was going to want more. She delighted his senses, but he had to be careful not to let himself be taken in. She was just a tourist, he reminded himself, and not a permanent resident. She could be a big headache if he didn't handle this right. Sometimes that act of hers almost fooled him, but no woman her age could be that innocent and ignorant of men. He had to keep that in mind.

Christy felt as if she'd done something unforgiveable. She wondered what had disturbed him, because she could feel him drawing away from her. She wrapped her arms across her breasts and stared quietly out the window all the way back.

He walked her to her cottage with a minimum of conversation, as silent as the palo verde trees that lined the walk.

She unlocked her door and turned on the light inside, turning to Nate with a question in her eyes.

"I'll see you in the morning," he remarked. He touched her cheek with his fingers and abruptly turned and walked away.

Christy went inside and closed the door. She felt as if he'd already closed one in her face, and she didn't even understand why.

George hovered at breakfast the next morning until she had to invite him to sit with her. At least he was consistent, she thought bitterly. Nate had gone out earlier on his way to work, apparently, and he'd spared her no more than a glance and a curt nod. His behavior was the most puzzling she'd ever seen.

"Did you have a good time with Mr. Lang last night?" George asked, a little too casually.

"It was all right," she said, downplaying it. She smiled at George over a forkful of scrambled eggs. "How was the chess game?"

"I won." He laughed. "First time, too. Mrs. Lang played several games with me. She's very nice."

"Yes, I like her, too. What are we going to do today?"

"More of the same thing we did yesterday," George said. "Archaeology is a very exacting science. I used to think it would be glamorous and adventurous to go searching for ancient ruins. Now that I've discovered you do most of the work with a sifting box and a toothbrush, it's lost a lot of its appeal. I think I'll stick to anthropology."

"Isn't that the same kind of thing?"

"Basically, but an anthropologist can go and live in Third World cultures that have their roots in the past. He can experience first-hand the kind of lives they live. Remember reading about Margaret Mead and all the exciting places she went? That's what I'd like to do."

"You could wind up in somebody's stewing pot in the jungle," she felt obliged to point out.

He shrugged. "Death is nothing more than transition from one plane of existence to another, Christy. Why be afraid of it?"

"That's a different way of thinking about it," she said, taken aback by his easy acceptance of something that was, to her, formidable.

"My parents were missionaries," he grinned. "I grew up in places where you could wind up in a stew pot. That's why I'm not afraid of it."

"Oh, I see." She smiled at him. "I guess your childhood was a lot more exciting than mine."

"You're from Jacksonville, aren't you?" he asked.

She nodded. "It's a great place to live. But I like Arizona," she added, and her eyes went dreamy.

George grimaced. It wasn't hard to see why she liked it. He sipped his orange juice and wondered why he couldn't be more dashing.

Later, Christy sat with him while they worked at the dig, poring over pottery pieces. He didn't know that her mind was on the way Nate Lang had kissed her the night before and his strange behavior afterward and today.

Nate didn't come around all day, and he wasn't at supper. Christy called Joyce Ann because she was bored and sad and nervous and needed to talk.

"Are you getting homesick?" her older sister asked hopefully.

"Not really," Christy began.

"Well, Harry must miss you. He's called three times already. Look, Christy, I know he leaves a lot to be desired, but he'd take good care of you…"

"I know that, Joyce Ann," she told the older woman gently.

She couldn't blame her sister for wanting to see her settled and secure. But Harry was not at all her idea of the husband she wanted to spend her life with.

"Tell me you aren't getting involved with that man you told me about," Joyce Ann said suddenly. "A holiday romance is one thing, but you won't do something silly like getting in over your head with a stranger, will you?"

Christy's heart jumped. Amazing, how easily her sister read her. "Of course not," she protested. "I mean, there are a lot of men out here. George works with me at the dig. He's a college senior and a very nice boy."

"But he isn't the one you've got your eye on. Who is?"

She gave in to the need to tell someone. "His name is Nathanial," she said. "He's a miner."

"Oh, my God! A caveman!"

Christy burst out laughing. "No! He works in an office, not down a mine shaft. He's tall and rugged-looking, and very smart. He has a huge computer."

"And money?" Joyce Ann asked shrewdly.

"He and his mother own this ranch," she said.

"A mama's boy!"

"No!" She shook her hair back. "Joyce Ann, he's a very mature—"

"How old?"

"I don't really know. I guess he's in his middle thirties."

"So is Harry."

"Harry is forty and paunchy and about as romantic as Jell-O!"

"Speaking for myself, I find Jell-O with whipped cream on top very romantic indeed."

Christy sat back in her chair, curling the telephone cord

around her fingers. "Harry doesn't love me, and I sure don't love him."

"Well, don't tell me you love the Arizona caveman," Joyce Ann scoffed, "because you don't fall in love in just a few days."

"Don't you?" Christy asked sadly. "I don't suppose it matters anyway, because he doesn't seem to feel that way about me. He takes me places and then goes off and ignores me."

"Does he?" There was new interest in her sister's voice. "Gets mad, does he?"

"He seems to stay that way. And he looks at me in the oddest way." She crossed her long legs. "Anyway, I don't suppose he'd be interested seriously in a schoolteacher from the East. He's rich and good-looking and has his pick of women. I don't imagine he has any trouble finding them, either. This ranch always has women guests, and most of them are rich."

"Rich doesn't buy love."

"So they say, but it makes it easier to digest, I'll bet. Joyce Ann, how would you like to hear about the *Hohokam*?"

"Not long-distance, darling, you'll go bankrupt. You can tell me about them when you come home. When are you coming home, Christy?"

"In another week," Christy replied, feeling already the pain of parting from Nate. She'd only known him for a few days, but it felt like years and she couldn't bear the thought of leaving him.

"Don't sound so morose. Harry says he's going to meet you at the airport with a dozen roses."

The thought of Harry with a dozen roses in his arms made her burst out laughing. She got Joyce Ann started, and then they began to reminisce about the old days, when their parents were still alive. Joyce Ann could be a pain, but it was so nice not to be alone in the world.

As she said good night and hung up, she wondered how she was going to manage if she had to go home and fight off Harry's practical proposal all over again.

Chapter Four

The next day was Saturday, and the team was given the weekend off. A trail ride was planned for guests at the ranch, along with a shopping trip to town, a small rodeo, and a camping trip that night in the mountains behind the ranch. It would be a full day, but all Christy saw were the regular wranglers. She hadn't even caught a glimpse of Nate, and some of the joy and excitement went out of the activities because he wasn't around.

George, of course, stuck to her like glue. He was delighted to have a partner for the trail ride. The only thing was, he apparently couldn't ride at all. He was allergic to horses and obviously terrified of them. What happened was probably inevitable, Christy thought as she watched the horse he was on begin to buck. George came off the horse, landing flat on his back in the dust, with the breath knocked out of him.

She and Mrs. Lang fussed over him while one of the men was delegated to take him to town to be X-rayed. He was limping a little, but Christy was almost sure no real damage had been done. George was just enjoying the attention he was getting. He asked her to ride into town with them, but before she could answer, Nate came striding up and appropriated her with only a brief sympathetic word to George and a nod to his mother.

"George is hurt," she protested.

"George is a blithering idiot," he said shortly. He glared down at her as he propelled her back toward the barn. "And I'll be damned if he's going to monopolize you with that fake fall."

"But it wasn't fake…!"

He turned her to him within sight of the other guests mounting their horses. "Listen. Your friend George hit hard, but he knew how to fall, surely you noticed that?"

She had noticed, although she hadn't suspected that George had done it on purpose. She stared up at Nate curiously.

He hated that look. He couldn't decide if she was sophisticated and trying to pretend she wasn't, or if that innocence was real. She was full of contradictions and he didn't know whether he was coming or going lately.

Frowning, he stared down at her, his eyes suddenly kindling as the look took on new dimensions, made her knees weak, her breath come in faint gasps. The magic was there again, as potent as ever.

"Where are we going?" she asked, trying to break the spell before she gave in to it again.

"Riding," he said.

"But, I can't…!"

"I'll teach you." He took her hand and led her into the stable where two of the cowboys were busily saddling horses for the guests. "Bud!" he called to one of them. "Saddle Blue for Christy."

"Yes, sir!"

The young cowboy moved toward an older horse, a palomino, and Christy watched with delight as it was saddled and led to her.

"This is Blue," Nate told her, thanking the cowboy as he took the reins. "Blue was my birthday present when I was fifteen. He's twenty-two now, and he doesn't get ridden much, but he likes a leisurely trail ride now and again. He's very gentle. He won't throw you."

She moved toward the horse and lifted a hesitant hand to his soft muzzle. He let her stroke him, his big brown eyes kind and watchful.

"Oh, he's beautiful!" Christy exclaimed. "What a nice boy," she cooed as she stroked his forehead. "Nice old fellow."

"Here, give him this and he'll be your friend for life. Mind your fingers, though." He handed her a sugar cube, which she fed to the horse. "We don't let him have much sugar these days. It isn't good for him to get overweight, but he's got a sweet tooth."

"I guess you could ride from the time you could sit up," she mused.

"Almost," he agreed. "My dad put me in the saddle when I was four and kept me there until I learned to ride the way he thought I should. He was a former rodeo star. His son had to be the best, at everything, on horseback."

The deep, angry note in his voice caught her attention. She looked up at him.

He laughed when he saw the way she was looking at him. "I'll bet your dad spoiled you rotten," he murmured.

"My parents died when I was twelve," she said. "Joyce Ann raised me. She's been more mother than big sister all my life."

He brushed the hair back from her face, gently. "My kids aren't going to be pushed into doing things they don't want to do," he said.

"Neither are mine," she replied.

He searched her eyes. "We're different in coloring," he murmured, lifting her hand in his to study it. "My skin is much darker than yours, like my hair and my eyes."

"I take after my mother," she said. "Her grandmother was Norwegian."

He smiled. "I take after my mother, too. Her mother was Spanish."

"I thought she might be. She's still very lovely."

"Yes." He let go of her hand, disturbed at the images that had been dancing around in his brain. He couldn't help but wonder if he and Christy had kids, which one of their parents the children would favor. Those weren't thoughts he should be considering. This was just a holiday romance, he told himself firmly.

He helped Christy into the saddle, trying not to laugh as she tugged and panted her way onto the horse with his help.

"My goodness, it's much harder than it looks on television!" she exclaimed.

"Oh, you should be overweight and try it," he murmured dryly. "Riding a horse is pretty easy compared to getting on and off one. It just takes practice."

She was still panting, pushing her hair out of her eyes. "I guess so."

"You shouldn't ride longer than an hour, either," he added as he went to get his own mount.

"Why?"

He swung into the saddle with the ease of years of practice and moved his horse up to hers. "Because you're going to discover that you use muscles you didn't know you had. By tonight you'll be walking bowlegged, and tomorrow you'll be stiff as a board."

She fingered the reins. "I don't suppose there's a van going to church?"

He chuckled. That was a nice touch, he thought to himself. She was really putting on the act for him. "No. Most of the guests like to sleep late on Sunday. But mother and I go, if you'd like to come."

She beamed. "Thanks."

His slate-gray eyes ranged over her face with pure mockery, but she was too far away to see the expression. All she saw was the smile. "Don't pull too hard on those reins."

He rode off ahead of her, more disturbed than he wanted to let on. If she'd been a hometown girl, if that pose of hers was real, she'd have been everything he'd ever wanted in a wife. As it was...

They headed around the valley and through a small canyon, and while they rode, he told her about the vegetation that grew in the desert and how it held water.

"Notice the leaves," he said, reining in, indicating one of the prickly pear cacti beside the trail. "If the leaves are fat, it means we've had rain. If they're skinny, we haven't. The leaves on desert plants usually stay thin during periods of drought so that the plant won't require as much moisture. Now, the saguaro is pleated, like an accordion, to allow it to expand with water when it rains." He crossed his forearms over each other on the pommel and stared at her. "Did you know that a saguaro can weigh up to ten tons? There's a skeleton inside it to support that weight, and most of it is just water. The saguaro doesn't grow an arm until it's from seventy to seventy-five years old. They can live to be two hundred years old."

She caught her breath. Just looking at the huge cacti in the Saguaro National Monument outside Tucson had fascinated her as they drove through the monument to get to the ranch. But Dr. Adamson hadn't known a lot about the giant cacti, so conversation had centered on the dig, not the vegetation.

"That's not a fraction of fact on the plants here," he mused, staring out over the desert. "My God, a botanist could spend his life learning about desert plants. The *Papago* use them for medicine, for food, for liquor. They make flour from the dried pods of palo verde and mesquite. They fry or boil the leaves on prickly pear cacti for food. They make a kind of beer from the fruit of the prickly pear and the saguaro. I could go on for hours."

"I could listen for hours," she replied. "I'd like to take pictures of those plants for my class back home. The children would enjoy learning about a different kind of vegetation than they're used to."

He frowned as he looked at her. If she really was an elementary school teacher—and everything pointed to it—that one fact didn't jibe with what he thought she was. If she led a wild life, wouldn't the education department protest? And how could she settle for such a tame career, if she was the pretty little flirt she'd convinced him she was? It didn't make sense.

"Why do you teach school?" he asked bluntly.

"I don't know. It just sort of fell into my lap. My father was a teacher. He loved the life, and I loved him." She smiled. "My mother was an artist. They were terribly mismatched, but it

was just as well they died together." The smile faded. "They
were so devoted to each other that one wouldn't have thrived
without the other. I suppose I've spent my whole life looking
for that kind of love, but maybe it's so rare that it only happens
for one couple out of ten thousand."

"Maybe," he agreed. "My parents never got along. My
father married my mother because he wanted this ranch. He
managed to drive it into bankruptcy with his extravagant ideas
of how to make an empire of it. He died when I was twenty-
five," he added curtly, and his dark eyes glittered. "He never
forgave me for preferring geology to ranching. When he
couldn't browbeat me into doing what he wanted, he tried
freezing me out. I don't think he said ten words to me after I
started college."

She wondered if he'd ever told anyone else that, and
decided that he was such a private person that he probably
hadn't. It flattered her that he felt so at ease with her. "Your
mother is very proud of you."

His dark gray eyes searched hers. "Yes. She was the one
person who ever cared enough to let me be myself." He pushed
back the creamy Stetson he was wearing. "Most women go
into a relationship with the idea that they'll change a man to
suit them. It's not that easy to restructure a person's personality, and not much of a man who'll allow a woman to do it."

"If you change people, sometimes you change the things
you love most about them, without realizing it," she replied.

He stared at her blatantly. She was beautiful with the sun
making a golden fire of her wavy hair as the wind moved it
around. Her pale green eyes were soft and warm as she looked
back at him, and there was an attractive color in her cheeks.
She was wearing a gaily striped blouse with puffy sleeves that

buttoned up the front with her tight jeans and tan boots, and she looked like the Eastern tourist she was. But she had a lovely figure and Nate remembered so well how she felt in his arms. Fires began to burn deep inside him as he looked at her. She knew the score, for God's sake, and she wanted him, too. He knew by the electricity that sparkled between them when they were alone. So why was he holding back?

His jaw clenched. He glanced past her to the shade of some palo verde trees by the wash that was, infrequently, a running stream during the rainy season. "Let's rest a bit," he said.

She followed him into the shady area and watched him tether his mount to a palo verde tree. He reached up to help her down from her own horse, deliberately letting her slide against him, so that she could feel the corded muscles in his body, feel the warm strength of it, feel his breath sighing heavily against her face as he helped her down.

The nearness was unnerving, especially when his dark eyes looked down into hers and time spun out between them.

"I'll tie Blue for you," he said huskily. "Then you and I are going to make love."

She wasn't quite sure she'd heard that last bit, because he turned away as he said it and probably she'd misunderstood. He tethered Blue and came back to her, and then she knew that she hadn't mistaken what he'd said. His eyes were blazing with raw desire.

He bent and lifted her easily in his muscular arms and carried her, holding her fascinated gaze, to the shelter of the tree. He laid her down in the soft sand and stretched out beside her, pausing just long enough to let his hat sail to one side before he bent to her mouth.

She knew then how much he'd been playing with her. The

teasing kisses of the past were totally eclipsed by the blatant, demanding hunger of the kiss he now gave her. His mouth was hard and rough, pushing her lips apart with fierce command, making her submit with the threatened pressure of his body while he deepened the kiss into something far beyond her slight experience.

"Relax," he said against her soft mouth. "There's nothing to be afraid of. I may be a little rougher than the men you're used to, but I won't hurt you."

That didn't make sense at first. Then she felt his tongue go into her mouth, felt his hands sliding under her top, against her bare skin. Her eyes flew open and she tried to speak, but his mouth grew rougher.

He moved, one long leg insinuating itself between both of hers, and she felt the power and strength of him in an embrace she'd never shared with a man before.

"Please...you're going...too fast!" she whispered, frightened.

He lifted his head, searching her eyes. He frowned, because she actually looked frightened. Odd, when she was such a pretty, outgoing woman. Men must have been camped on her doorstep for years now, and she surely didn't reach her present age without some experience. Not the way she looked. It must be part of the act, but that fear seemed real.

"How old are you, Christy?" he asked, his voice deep and faintly husky with desire. He knew, but he asked anyway.

"I'm twenty-five," she said uneasily.

His fingers were against her ribcage, gently caressing her so that unknown sensations began to work in her body. He made her feel odd, uneasy, excited, especially when he worked his way up to the band of her bra just under her breasts and lingered there. She shouldn't let him touch her this way, but something was happening to her that she didn't understand.

"I'm thirty-seven," he murmured, holding her eyes while that hand moved again and his fingers touched her breast, making her jump. "We're both plenty old enough to know what we're doing, aren't we?" he added.

"I...guess so," she managed. Her heart leaped. He was touching her, his fingers warm through the thin fabric of her bra, and she lay there docilely, letting him caress her. She couldn't imagine why she was permitting the intimacy, except that it was making her head spin and her body blaze up with pleasure. She made an odd sound and raised her back, shocking herself with the sensuous little movement.

He smiled, bending to her mouth again. "That's more like it," he whispered. "I wondered how long you could keep up the act..."

Her thoughts dissolved as his mouth covered hers again. His thumb rubbed over her nipple and she felt it tighten until it was almost painful, but every time he touched it, her body flinched with helpless pleasure. She moaned, tangling her hands in the hair at the nape of his neck, pulling his hard mouth even closer against her own. She opened her lips for him, inviting the thrust of his tongue into the soft, warm darkness of her mouth.

Fever, she thought while she could. It burned like a vicious fever. She wanted to be closer to him. She wanted to be without her clothing so that he could cool her hot skin by touching it with his lean, strong hands. She wanted his touch as she'd never wanted anything.

He seemed to know it, too, because he lifted her and snapped the fastening of her bra. Then he looked into her eyes and slid his hand over her naked breast, watching the expression that washed over her face.

"Yes, it's good, isn't it?" he asked gruffly. "Feeling my hands on your body, my mouth on your mouth. And this is just the beginning. Hasn't it been like this before?"

"No," she whispered brokenly. She shivered as he began to raise the hem of her blouse.

"There isn't another soul within twenty miles of us," he breathed, letting his eyes slide down to the bareness of her white skin as he pushed the offending fabric away and left her bare to the collarbone. His breath caught at the sight of her pretty breasts, pink-tipped, firm and peach-colored. He couldn't get enough of the sight of her. But it wasn't enough. Not nearly enough. He bent his head and opened his mouth, taking her inside.

Christy wept. It was the sweetest agony she'd ever known. His eyes on her body, the expression on his face that told her she was beautiful to him, the feel of his mouth against her tender skin. She clung to him, arching herself up to his lips, begging for the feel of them on her body. She thought she wouldn't survive the pleasure, and then he turned her into him and brought her hips against his with one fierce jerk of his lean hand.

She'd never experienced the feel of a man's aroused body. It terrified her. She cared for him and she didn't want to ask him to stop, but it was going to be too late if she waited much longer. Judging by the feel of him, and the faint shudder of his powerful body, he wasn't going to be too eager to stop anyway. He was sophisticated and he seemed to feel that she was, too. She didn't understand why he was letting things go this far. She'd told him she was a greenhorn, but perhaps he'd misunderstood.

She had to force her lips not to cling when he lifted his head. She could imagine how she looked, with her mouth swollen and her body half bare to his eyes. It was agony to stop.

"Please," she whispered, putting a trembling hand against his broad chest.

"Unbutton it," he said, his voice rough, his eyes glittering with desire.

"What?"

He snapped open the buttons, disclosing a chest thick with curly black hair. "Here." He dragged one of her hands to the hard, warm muscles and buried her fingers in the thick hair. "This is what I like," he breathed, moving her hand against him, groaning at the delicious touch.

She felt her other hand joining the first one, too entranced by the forbidden delight to deny it to her starving senses. She touched him, fascinated with the way he felt under her hands, the wiry abrasion of hair tickling her fingers. He arched under her touch, just as she had under his, and she caught her breath to know that she could give back the pleasure he was showing her.

"Christy," he groaned. He bent to her mouth, dragging her body against his so that they melted together, skin against hair-roughened skin.

She cried out at the surge of feverish pleasure the contact gave her, at the hunger it rekindled to feel his aroused body so close to hers. But when he rolled her onto her back and moved over her, trapping her beneath his powerful legs, she panicked.

Her eyes flew open. "No!" she whispered shakily, meeting his hot gaze. "No, Nate, please! I can't!"

"Can't, the devil," he said, his voice biting as he stared down at her, on fire with the need to bury himself in her. "You can stop playing. You don't have to ply me with virginal wiles. I want you like hell."

"It isn't…playing," she said. "I'm a virgin."

He laughed coldly. "At your age? The way you look? Like hell you are!" He bent to kiss her again.

But she turned her face away. "I didn't always look like this! Nate, I've never…done this!" she said frantically. "You don't understand!"

"Do you expect me to believe that?" he demanded, jerking her face back to his furious eyes. "My God, you've teased and flirted and had one 'accident' after another to get my attention. You've thrown yourself at me ever since you got here, so why act shocked when I make a move on you? You want me. I've known that from the first."

She bit her lower lip, so horribly embarrassed that she could hardly get the words out. He still had her pinned and now his arousal was becoming a terrible punishment.

"Yes, I wanted you," she confessed miserably. "But I thought…I thought you felt something for me."

He glared down at her, furious with her and with himself for what she was doing to him. "Felt something?" He laughed coldly. "Can't you feel what I want?" he asked with cruel mockery and moved his hips deliberately against her, watching the flaming color come into her face. "Yes, you know what that is, don't you? Why pretend it's such a shocking experience?"

"Because it is." She swallowed and closed her eyes, wishing she could just disappear. Her hands clenched on his shoulders. "Until a week ago, I looked like somebody's old maid aunt. I got my hair done and bought new clothes and…and revamped my personality. I thought for once in my life, I'd try to be like those women I admired on television. You know, the independent, sophisticated, outgoing women that men…that men want." Tears welled in her eyes. "I didn't know, didn't realize, that I'd be mistaken for a…for a tramp!"

Her voice broke and it finally got through to him that he was treating her like one.

His lean hand jerked her face back up to his while his body throbbed in anguish over hers. "Are you serious?" he asked curtly. "Are you really trying to convince me that you're a virgin? That you've never been intimate with a man?"

"Nobody ever wanted to be intimate with somebody who looked like I did," she whispered, her voice shaking as she met his accusing dark eyes. His weight was formidable and she just wanted to get away from him. He looked as if he hated her. "I was just a dull little dishwater blonde. I had my hair lightened and my face done, I bought new makeup and new clothes and forced myself to try and be outgoing. I thought…" She closed her eyes. "I thought maybe if I were pretty, men might notice me. I've been alone all my life. I just wanted somebody to love me," she whispered in a fever of embarrassment.

His jaw clenched. It sounded too genuine to be a lie, but he hated her for what he was hearing. "Love is a rare commodity," he said tersely, easing his body away from hers. "I don't have any to give. All I wanted was one night with you, Christy, not happy ever after. I'm thirty-seven. If I wanted to be married, believe me, I could be."

"Yes, I know that," she said. She heard him move away and she managed to sit up without looking at him, embarrassed at her disheveled clothing, at the way she'd responded to him. Her trembling fingers gathered the fabric to her taut, swollen breasts. She could still feel his mouth on them, like a brand.

"I can't believe a woman could be that green," he said, his voice cutting as he glared down at her, trying to get his breath. "Surely you knew what I was leading up to? The way you kept stumbling around me, the way you smiled and teased, added to the way you looked was enough to make any man want you."

"Yes. Well, I didn't know that," she managed. She sighed miserably. "I'm sorry. I just wanted someone to love me."

He looked at her with pure fury, his fists clenched at his sides while he breathed unsteadily. "And all I wanted was a little sex," he said coldly, forcing himself to say the words, to make her understand. It was cruel, he knew it, but it would be the kindest thing in the long run. He didn't want commitment. All he'd wanted was a night in her arms, but he hadn't bargained for this! "If you want love and marriage, honey, you won't find either one with me. I thought you were in the market for a holiday romance, and I was willing to oblige. My mistake."

What she saw in his face made her feel ashamed. She averted her eyes from the condemnation of his, embarrassed and wounded. Her hands trembled as she got her bra and blouse back on and scrambled to her feet. She brushed the sand from her jeans without looking at him. She couldn't say anything, because her mind had stopped working.

He hated her. He hated himself. He glared at her trembling body and wanted to throw things. Why hadn't he realized that it was no act? No experienced woman would have behaved as she had, and no actress was good enough to keep up the masquerade so consistently. It was no act. She really was a virgin. Imagine that, he thought furiously. A real live innocent who looked like she did. She'd said something about changing her image, but he couldn't imagine that she'd been less than beautiful before.

Then a terrible thought occurred to him. He tried to push it away, but it wouldn't go.

"How are you set financially?" he asked bluntly.

"I teach school. How do you think I'm set?" she asked miserably. She pushed back her disheveled hair. Her eyes lifted to his. "What difference does it make?"

"None, now that I've found you out," he replied coolly. "I'm rich. I guess the money really appealed to you, didn't it?"

She gaped at him. Could he honestly believe that? Probably he could. He seemed to enjoy thinking the worst of her today. Maybe it made him feel better. She was aware that getting stirred up was painful to men, and he'd been pretty stirred.

She turned away, toward her horse. "I'd like to go back now," she said in a defeated tone.

"We might as well," he agreed curtly. "You've had your shot at the brass ring, but you fell a little short, didn't you, honey?"

She cringed at the mockery in his tone. She loved him, and he could treat her like this, with such coldness. It was just as well that she'd found out now, before she let herself hope for anything more. He wanted sex, not love, and she wasn't capable of a purely physical liaison. What irony. She'd come to Arizona looking for love, and she'd found a man with a heart as barren as the desert he lived in.

She let him help her into the saddle, noticing absently that he'd fastened his shirt back up. She didn't want to remember how his chest had felt under her caressing hands, or how his mouth had felt on her body. She had to put it into perspective. It had been physical attraction, nothing more. He didn't want her for keeps, he just wanted to make love to her. She sighed wearily. If that was all he wanted, then why hadn't he just left her alone? It would have been kinder for both of them if he'd never touched her.

He swung into the saddle, disturbed by his own feelings of guilt. He'd been the pursuer, not she, despite the accusations he'd made. He should have known how green she was and left her to George. Damn it, he'd backed her into a corner and then attacked her for refusing to let him use her. He was vaguely ashamed of his own behavior. But he didn't want to get married, he told himself firmly. He'd escaped the noose too many times already to voluntarily put his head into it now. No, he'd get over Christy and she'd get over him. It was just one of those unfortunate interludes that was best forgotten.

"Don't look so dismal," he said, riding along beside her as they headed back. "We'll forget it happened."

She didn't answer him. She didn't want to look at him or talk to him ever again. It might not be a mature attitude to take, but she didn't feel very mature. She felt cheap and ashamed. Perhaps he was right, and she had led him on with her false image. Perhaps men looked at things differently than women did, and her pretty appearance gave the impression, along with her unfortunate clumsiness and teasing, that she was "available."

Joyce Ann was right, she decided. She should go home and marry Harry and settle down. This disguise she'd adopted was nothing like the woman she really was, and she should be ashamed for giving a false impression. Starting tomorrow, the old Christy was going to be very much back in her proper place. She wasn't going to hurt anyone else with her stupid ideas of changing. Besides, she thought sadly, she couldn't change, not really. She wasn't vivacious and outgoing and beautiful. She was serious and introverted and plain. She'd do well to remember it from now on. Nathanial Lang didn't want her as she appeared to be, then he certainly wouldn't want her as she was. It had been a lucky escape for both of them.

He glanced at her, disturbed because she wouldn't answer him. She looked…devastated. He dragged his eyes back to the trail in front of them. He shouldn't have been so cruel to her. She was more sensitive than he'd realized.

"Christy…" he began.

"It's all right, Mr. Lang," she said gently. She didn't look at him, but at the reins in her hands. "I'm sorry for everything. I won't bother you anymore, I promise."

"Oh, for God's sake…!" he raged.

She would have burst into tears at his tone, but a party of riders approaching cut into the tense silence between them and she gave a huge sigh of relief when she saw George. Sanctuary, she thought, heading old Blue in his direction. George had recovered enough to come on the trail ride, and Christy was going to stick to him like glue, she promised herself. At least George only wanted companionship, not to get her into bed!

Nate watched her ride away with mixed feelings. It looked as if George was going to get her after all. Just as well, he assured himself. He had nothing to offer her. George was steady and dependable.

Nate lifted his chin and glared as the younger man beamed when Christy joined him. Damn it all, he thought furiously, life had been so simple before this archaeology outfit pushed itself into his privacy. Now he was confused and hurt and he didn't know what he wanted anymore. He wheeled his own mount with a silent curse and rode away, leaving his foreman to conduct the group on its trail ride without him. He couldn't stand the pain in Christy's soft eyes one more minute!

Chapter Five

Christy was never as glad to see anyone as she was to see George. She rode up beside him and stuck like glue, trying not to notice the abrupt way Nate Lang made his departure. She was still shaking inside from what had happened.

"Are you all right?" George asked when they stopped to water the horses on the mountain trail.

"Of course," she said brightly, brushing back her disheveled hair.

"You look funny," he said, frowning. "Upset."

"I almost fell off my horse," she lied. "It unnerved me. But I'm all right now. Are you?" she added, remembering his fall.

He smiled sheepishly and adjusted his glasses, an action that Christy found all too familiar, as they slipped down his nose. "Well, actually, that was a planned fall. I'm good with horses, but I thought you might notice if I got hurt."

"Of course I noticed," she chided gently.

He cleared his throat, toying with his horse's reins and looking at them instead of her. "Christy, I like you…a lot."

"I like you, too, George," she said gently. She put a hand on his forearm. Nathanial Lang was right, she thought as she studied the flustered young man. It was better to be honest with people. "George, I have to tell you that I'm going to be married when I go back to Jacksonville. I hadn't made up my mind when I came out here, but I sort of had it made up for me."

He looked wounded for a moment, then he got himself back together and straightened. "I'm sorry, for myself. He'll be a lucky man. Have you known him long?" he added, and forced a smile.

"Since I started teaching," she said. "He teaches sixth grade at the elementary school where I work. He's…he's a good bit older than I am. He's divorced and he has three sons. They're all in high school, but they like me and I like them."

He tried not to show how dismayed he felt. Surely Christy deserved better than that! "You'll have one big family, what with his kids and the ones you'll have together," he said cheerfully.

She seemed to wither before his eyes. She even looked momentarily older. "Oh, Harry doesn't want any more children," she said. "He's made sure he won't have any, so there's no question of…" She turned away, hating the thought of never holding a child of her own in her arms. It was too painful to think about. "We'd better go."

George helped her to mount and then got on his own horse. What she told him was enough to keep him depressed all the way back to the ranch.

Christy refused to go on the overnight camp out. Nate went, and she was glad to have the recreation room pretty much to herself. She was so engrossed in a book that she hardly heard Mrs. Lang come in and sit down across from her.

"You'd have enjoyed the camp, Christy," the small woman said, smiling at her gently. "It's quite something, the campfire on the desert and the taste of freshly brewed camp coffee. Our foreman, Terrance, plays guitar and he has a marvelous voice."

"I didn't really feel up to it," she said, and it was the truth in several ways. "I got pretty sore from the ride earlier today."

Mrs. Lang's dark eyes were persistent as they searched the younger woman's face. "Nate hasn't said two words all day. He snapped at me when I asked if he was going camping, and he stayed in his study until it was time to leave. When he found out you weren't going along, he used language I won't even repeat. It got worse when George volunteered to stay behind with you. I think Nate might have roped and dragged him with them if he hadn't changed his mind."

Christy flushed, fumbling with the book. "George is a nice boy. But I explained things to him this afternoon. I had to make him understand that…well, that there was no chance of our being more than friends."

Mrs. Lang smiled. "I had an idea that you'd have to speak to him eventually. I assume your affections are engaged elsewhere?" she fished delicately.

Christy nodded. "I'm getting married when I go back to Florida."

Mrs. Lang dropped her dishcloth and bent to pick it up, her expression astonished. "I had no idea that you were engaged," she said haltingly.

"I'm not," Christy told her. "I came out here to think things over. I changed the way I look, but not the way I think and feel," she added sadly, lifting a ravaged expression to the older woman. "I'm still old-fashioned and full of hang-ups and unsuited to the modern world."

"In other words, you don't sleep around."

In spite of herself, Christy laughed at the twinkle in the other woman's eyes. "No, I don't sleep around," she agreed. She leaned back against the sofa. "Men don't really want marriage anymore. They don't need it unless they want children or belong to some conservative organization that likes settled executives. It's not that easy for even a pretty woman to find a husband, but it's doubly hard for an unattractive one. I can't live a breezy, rootless existence with only a career for comfort. I want a home of my own and children, even if they aren't my own," she said firmly, for her own benefit. "I'm twenty-five. If I don't marry while I have the chance, it might never come again." She looked up. "I don't want to live alone until I die."

"Tell me about this man you've decided to marry."

Christy did, her eyes dull and lackluster. "He's almost forty," she added. "But he's a kind man, and he'll give me security and a good life."

"Do you love him?"

"I'm very fond of him," Christy said hesitantly.

"Do you want him?"

She thought of Nate's mouth on hers, his hands holding her against him with passionate need, and she closed her eyes. "I can endure that part of the marriage."

"Oh, my dear," Mrs. Lang sighed heavily. "My dear, it's more than just endurance. Men know when you feel nothing. It will hurt your husband. Eventually, it will kill your marriage. It isn't fair to either of you to marry without desire."

"The way my life is going, I can have either but not both,"

she said with a humorless laugh. She looked up. "Mrs. Lang, I've done a bad thing. I've pretended to be something I'm not, and now I'm having to pay for it. I wish I'd stayed at home and been satisfied with what I had."

"If everyone took that attitude, America would never have been discovered," Mrs. Lang returned. She leaned forward and patted Christy's hand. "Don't worry so, child. Let each day take care of itself. You still have a week to go, you know."

"I thought I might go home Monday…"

"No!" Mrs. Lang stood up. "Don't you dare. Running away from a problem never solved it. Besides, you've already paid for your holiday. The least you can do is stay and enjoy it."

Christy wasn't sure that it was the right thing to do, but in her heart, she didn't want to leave Nate yet. She wondered if his mother had guessed how she felt about him. She was a wise little woman with keen eyes, and she didn't miss much. It was flattering that his mother didn't want her off the Lang ranch. Since she didn't, it blew up Joyce Ann's theory that Nate was a mother's boy. No, he wasn't. Not by a long shot. But he would never be Christy's, either. He'd as much as said so. Every day she remained here would be painful and too long. But running wasn't really her style, either.

"I suppose I should stay," Christy said finally. "It would leave the others in a bind if I go early." She forced a smile. "And you're right. Running doesn't really solve things, I guess."

"That sounds more like it," the older woman replied. "Now I have to get back to my dishes. Why don't you have an early night? Nate mentioned that you wanted to go to church with us in the morning?"

"If you don't mind, Mrs. Lang, I think I'll pass. This time," she added, trying not to give too much away.

But Mrs. Lang was shrewd. She had a fairly good idea of what had happened. "I understand. Another time, perhaps. Goodnight, Christy."

Christy smiled gently. "Goodnight."

She knew it was cowardly to back out of church because she couldn't face Nate after what had happened the day before, but it was too much to ask. She was too ashamed of herself. He said that she'd led him on, and maybe she had. She hadn't realized that she was doing it, that was what made it so terrible. She was a greenhorn, all right, in just about every respect.

She got up the next morning after a sleepless night fraught with erotic, violent dreams that kept her tossing all over the bed until dawn. She dragged herself up and took a shower. Then she glared at herself in the mirror, wondering if she shouldn't go whole hog with her repentance and turn herself back into the pitiful wallflower she'd been before she came out here. But that would be silly, she decided, and it wouldn't bother Nate. It would just make people feel sorry for her, and that was the last thing she wanted. But she didn't go to a lot of trouble with the careful makeup she'd used before, and she didn't spend half an hour curling her hair with the styling rod.

She decided to give breakfast a miss, because she might run into Nate. Then she decided to give lunch a miss for the same reason. She had some cookies in her purse. She ate those and drank some water, hating her own cowardice. This wasn't like her, really it wasn't, but her pride and her heart had never been crushed so terribly.

When she didn't come out for lunch, Nate was disturbed because he knew she hadn't had breakfast. She couldn't starve herself, for God's sake! He felt more guilty by the minute for the way he'd hurt her the day before. He should have been a little less cruel, but then, hindsight was a great asset. He wondered how he was going to bear being around her for the rest of her stay, seeing that hurt look in her eyes and knowing he'd put it there. But then, she shouldn't have flirted with him so much, he told himself. And there was still the matter of those clumsy antics to get his attention. She'd asked for it. He had to keep believing that, or he was going to go crazy.

He went into the dining room where guests were going through the buffet line and started to fill a plate for her when he encountered George holding two.

"I thought I'd take Christy something," he told Nate. "She's feeling kind of low. I guess the man back home called and upset her or something, because she was really depressed yesterday. I don't think she's even come out of her room. I haven't seen her at all."

Nate felt as if he'd been frozen in his boots. "The man back home?" he prompted.

"The one she's going to marry," George said miserably. "He's forty and settled, and she says he'll look after her— Here, Mr. Lang, you're about to spill that chicken…"

Nate set the plate on the table and walked out of the room without speaking. He found himself, eventually, out on the desert behind the ranch, standing bareheaded in a stand of spreading creosote bushes in the dirt. The wind whipped through his hair and he felt it, but it hardly registered. Christy was going home to marry someone. She'd been engaged all along and she hadn't told him. She'd let him take her out and make love to her, and then she'd fought free and started spouting excuses.

Was she a virgin? Or was it just guilty conscience because she was betraying the man she'd promised herself to? He

wanted to jerk up a creosote bush and beat the desert with it.
It might help alleviate some of his bad temper. The woman was
driving him crazy! Well, let her go home and marry her settled
man, he didn't care! He'd be glad when she was out of his hair
and in someone else's, he told himself. Of course he would!

He was so angry and irritable that he locked himself in his
study for the rest of the day and didn't even go in to the office.
In fact, he didn't even stop working to eat. Let her marry her
settled fool. He didn't give a damn.

Christy avoided the house all day, having an early night.
Bless George for bringing her food, because she'd rather have
starved than have to face Nate until she'd gotten her nerves
settled. George had admitted that he'd told Nate about Harry,
and she imagined what Nate was thinking now. He probably
had a good picture of her as a two-timing Jezebel. She
couldn't win for losing, she thought miserably.

Sure enough, Nate looked at her the next morning as if he
hated the sight of her. She was wearing her jeans and a white
embroidered smock top for coolness and comfort. She'd put
her hair up and she hadn't used any makeup at all. But if she'd
hoped to look plain again she didn't succeed. Her face looked
young and innocent with her clear complexion, and her hair
in its soft bun, leaving her nape bare, gave her a vulnerable
air. Nate found her every bit as attractive now as he had when
she worked at her makeup and her hairdo and dressed to the
hilt. That made him feel even worse. He strode toward his car
and went to his office without one single word to her, or to
anyone else.

George stuck with her when they went out to the dig, en-
couraging and kind. Why, oh, why couldn't she have given

her heart to him? He wouldn't throw it in the sand and stomp on it the way Nate had!

It was a long day, as Mondays always seemed to be, and the heat was oppressive. She was glad when they were able to go back to the ranch to have lunch under the palo verde trees. But when they got there, everything was in a frenzy. Mrs. Lang was nowhere in sight and one of the maids was trying to set the buffet table, muttering to herself in rapid-fire Spanish.

"What's wrong?" Christy asked gently.

But the answer came in Spanish and Christy had only a little French to her credit. She smiled apologetically, going out to sit with George.

Mrs. Lang, looking harassed and haunted, came out of the house just as everyone lined up for the buffet.

"What's wrong?" Christy asked gently.

"Nate," came the reply. "There was a cave-in at one of the mines this morning. He was in it when it happened, part of an executive tour."

Christy went stark white. "Is he alive?" she asked, her voice shaking.

Mrs. Lang studied the young face for a long moment and then she smiled gently and touched the thin shoulder. "Yes, he's alive. Very much alive. Just a little bruised and scratched, but the doctor wanted him to spend the rest of the day in bed, to make sure there are no complications."

"Oh, thank God." Christy bit back tears, embarrassed at the way she'd blown her cover. She shook her head to clear the tears, glad that she and Mrs. Lang were standing apart from the archaeological group, so that no one could see her face.

"I've got to go to town and get some prescriptions filled

for him," the older woman said with a calculating stare. "Could you sit with him for me?"

"He wouldn't like that, Mrs. Lang," Christy said quietly. "It would be better if you asked someone else."

"No, I don't think so." She took Christy by the hand and led her firmly down the hall and into Nate's room, where he lay smoldering in his bed with his chest bare and the sheet lying precariously across his lean hips.

"I've asked Miss Haley to sit with you while I go to town for your prescriptions, Nate," Mrs. Lang said, pretending innocence. "I'll have Nita bring a tray so you can have lunch while I'm gone. I won't be long."

She was out the door before Christy could argue any more, before Nate could voice the words hanging on the tip of his tongue. He glared at Christy from cold slate eyes, a slash across his forehead and another across his cheek making him look even more dangerous than before. The gashes had been treated with antiseptic, and the one on his forehead was stitched. It would probably leave a scar. There was a bandage on one shoulder, white against the dark tan of his skin. He looked bruised and a little groggy, but formidable just the same.

"I'm sure one of the men wouldn't mind sitting with you…" she began hesitantly, so shy with him that it was painful just to talk to him.

"Sit down," he said. "I won't bite."

She colored as she slid into the chair near the bed, sitting stiffly on the very edge of it with her hands folded in her lap.

He studied her with more interest than he wanted to show, from the color in her cheeks to the rapid movement of her blouse. He made her nervous. He could see her eyes darting reluctantly over his bare, hair-roughened chest and away, as if the sight of him fascinated her. Once it would have amused him, even flattered him. But now he knew the truth about her, and he hated her attention.

"What's his name?" he asked, drawing up one knee under the white sheet to rest his wrist on.

"His...name?" she faltered.

"The man who's waiting for you back home. The one you're going to marry," he returned, his voice cutting.

"Oh. Him." She looked down at her hands. "His name is Harvey White, but most people call him Harry. He's forty, he teaches sixth grade, and he's...settled and mature."

He was also fifteen years older than she was, he thought angrily. Too old. Of course, he himself was twelve years her senior. He pushed that thought to the back of his mind and glared at her.

"A bachelor?"

"No," she replied. "He was married. His wife left him to marry another man. He has three teenaged sons. They're very nice," she added helplessly.

His jaw tautened as he stared at her. "A ready-made family. What about your own kids, how will they fit in?"

"We won't have any," she said, refusing to look at him. "Harry had an operation. He...doesn't want any more children, he said three was enough for us to look after financially."

"Oh, my God," he ground out. "You little fool, is that what you want?"

She lifted her face, aware that most of the color had drained out of it. She had a little pride left. "I'll have a secure life. I might not have made a good mother. Some women aren't cut out for it."

He was certain that she was. There was a nurturing quality

about her, a tenderness, that a child would sense and respond to. He hated the thought that she wouldn't have children. It wounded him.

"There are other men in the world," he said shortly.

"No, I don't think so," she said sadly. She smiled. "I'll be fine, Mr. Lang, you don't need to be concerned about me."

"Don't call me that," he said, his voice harsh as he stared at her. "My name is Nate."

She didn't know how to answer that, but she didn't have to. Nita brought in the tray and set it on the table by Nate's bed. There was coffee and tea and cups with cream and sugar, a platter of cold cuts, salad and dressing and fruit, with two plates and utensils so that Christy could make whatever combination they wanted.

Nate spoke to the little Mexican woman in her own tongue, very fluently. She laughed and left them.

"I want coffee, black, and salad with ham and cheese and Thousand Island dressing," he said, leaning back on his pillows.

She almost smiled at his assertive tone. He was, at least, consistent. He never pulled his punches, even when he ordered lunch. She fixed his plate and handed it to him, putting his coffee cup and saucer within easy reach.

She fixed herself a fruit salad and coffee, also black, and went to sit in her chair.

They ate in a companionable silence. When they finished, she collected the plates and stacked them on the tray, then poured second cups of coffee.

"How did the cave-in happen?" she asked.

"Damned if I know. One minute the ceiling was overhead, the next I was wearing half of it," he said simply. His dark eyes narrowed as he searched her face. "I don't spend a lot of time in the mines, but the occasional inspection is a necessary part of my work."

"Yes, I suppose it would be," she said. She sipped her coffee.

"I don't like your hair like that, Christy," he said unexpectedly.

She steadied the cup that was trembling in her hands. "I'm sorry, but I don't wear it to suit you."

"Christy." He said her name, savoring it. "What's it short for?"

"Christiana," she said. "I was named for my grandmother."

"It's pretty." He stared at her until she felt like a butterfly on a pin. "Get up and close the door, Christiana," he said, his voice husky. Despite what he knew about her—perhaps even because of it—she stirred him to his bones. He wanted nothing more than the feel, the taste of her. It was suddenly exciting to know that no other man had touched her. He knew instinctively that even this man she was going to marry had never been allowed the intimacies he had. It made him feel a foot taller.

"I won't," she said quietly. She closed her eyes, so that the sight of him that way, his skin dark against the white sheets, his face sensually inviting, wouldn't tempt her. He had nothing to offer except an affair, and she wasn't built for affairs, even with a man she'd grown to love.

"Afraid of me?" he asked, his voice deep and soft and slow as he watched her.

She lifted her haunted eyes to his. "Please stop it," she asked softly. "I can't play the game. I'm not brave enough."

He wasn't taking no for an answer. His lean fingers went to the sheet and he smiled at her in a way that made her nerves leap. "Close the door, or you're going to get an eyeful," he said, and moved the sheet so that it inched down his ribcage.

She couldn't believe he'd do it, but she knew he didn't make threats. "That's not fair," she accused.

"Live dangerously. I might only want to talk."

"Really?" she asked in disbelief.

"Are you that conceited?" he murmured, letting his eyes run over her as if she hardly interested him at all. "You really aren't that desirable, honey," he lied.

She flinched and got to her feet. "All right," she replied. He'd cut her pride to the bone, but she wasn't going to let the hurt show. She went to the door and started to go through it.

"Do it," he threatened, "and I'll follow you, just as I am."

That would be interesting, she thought, having a naked man follow her out to the tables. But they were all men out there and she was the only person who was likely to get embarrassed.

She closed the door firmly and turned, leaning back against it. "You're no gentleman," she said shortly.

"That's a fact. Come here."

She hesitated. But he stared at her and the sheet inched down again.

"It's blackmail!" she accused. But she went, her face scarlet. She could see enough to embarrass her already, despite the fact that he was a little blurry at a distance.

"And I thought you were sophisticated," he said, shaking his head as she approached him warily. "My God, I was blind as a bat, wasn't I? It sticks out all over you."

"What does?" she queried.

He caught her hand and jerked her down beside him on the bed. "Your chastity," he said. He drew her hand to his hair-covered chest and pressed it there. "Take your hair down."

"Please…"

"Come on, honey," he said gently. "There's nothing to be

afraid of. Mother won't be gone that long, and I'm not going to do anything you'll be ashamed of later. Okay?"

She still didn't quite trust him, but his nearness was working on her will power. Again. She lifted her hands to her hair and let it loose, so that it curved gracefully around her shoulders.

He reached up. His strong hands lifted and turned her across him, so that she was lying beside him on the cool, crisp sheets.

"Nate, don't," she whispered, her eyes pleading with him.

"Life is too short to settle for crumbs, Christiana," he said quietly. His eyes fell to her soft mouth. "I want the whole cake." His mouth settled gently on hers, probing, coaxing her lips to open for him, so that he could taste their warm fullness. He arched over her, one hand sliding under her back to lift her even closer while the kiss grew slower and harder and then, deeper.

She stiffened. His head lifted and he looked down into her eyes.

"Why are you afraid of that?" he asked softly. "Deep kisses won't make you pregnant."

"I don't…want to be that intimate with you," she said miserably. "You're just playing!"

His fingers curled into her thick hair and tugged. "Like hell I'm just playing," he murmured. "Has Harry held you like this?" he asked suddenly. His slate eyes blazed up dangerously and his hand tightened in her hair. "Answer me. Has he?"

"No, but…"

"Have you let him touch you the way I did the other afternoon?" he persisted.

"Please, you're hurting my hair."

"I want to know if you've been intimate with him," he breathed roughly.

"I don't…feel like that with Harry," she blurted out.

He could feel himself tautening, but with pure pleasure, not with anger. He searched her face with eyes that glittered. "And you're going to marry him?" he asked coldly.

"I'll learn," she said mutinously.

He touched her soft mouth with his free hand, bending over her with silent intent. "You don't learn desire," he said softly. "Either it's there or it isn't. You feel it for me, don't you?"

She reddened. "I won't stay here and let you…Nate!" she gasped.

"You won't what?" he asked, as his hand smoothed deliberately down her body, trespassing under the waistband of her jeans to stroke her smooth, flat belly. "Go ahead. Tell me."

But she couldn't. Her mind was in limbo. She stared up at him helplessly, too entranced to even struggle.

He liked that helplessness. His hand smoothed back up, under her embroidered smock top to the lacy covering of her bra. He traced the whirl of lace, watching her face color, feeling her breath quicken.

"This is what you like most, isn't it?" he murmured, and his hand slid gently under the lace, to touch her bare skin, to trace the hard nipple that was screaming her response. "You like me to touch you here. But you like my mouth more than my hands, don't you, Christiana?" he whispered, bending. "Even through the fabric, it drives you mad…"

It did. She whimpered at the feel of his mouth on her. Her fingers clung to his thick hair and she shivered with the fire-hot brand of his mouth even through two layers of cloth.

"To hell with this," he ground out. He found the fastening underneath her and pushed the offending barrier out of his way, jerking up her smock so that he could find her with his mouth.

It had never been like this, so intense, so heated. She felt the hungry mouth fasten on her breast and she began to weep with reaction. The pleasure was almost pain in its intensity. She clung to him, pressing closer, begging for his touch.

He lifted his head, pausing to look down at his handiwork with blazing eyes before he lifted his gaze to lock with hers. She looked loved, he thought dazedly. Her misty pale green eyes were half-closed, her face a study in absolute surrender. He thought he'd never seen anything half as lovely in his life.

"Can Harry give you that?" he asked huskily.

"Don't," she pleaded in a broken whisper. "Don't...play with me. I can't help it."

He let out a rough sigh. "You might not believe it, but neither can I." He rolled away from her, his face hard and drawn.

She turned her head and only then noticed that the sheet had come away. He was as beautiful as a sculpture, all long elegant lines and powerful muscle. Even where he was most a man, he was beautiful. She couldn't see him with a great deal of clarity, but her eyes found him fascinating, dark skin with a tangle of black hair all over him, the very epitome of masculinity.

He felt her eyes and turned his head, watching her gaze wash over him. It aroused him to see her pleasure in his nudity, and the arousal took a physical form that she saw with dawning realization and then flaming embarrassment.

"You don't have to be afraid of it," he said gently when she averted her gaze jerkily. "It's a reaction I can't help, but I won't hurt you."

"I've never seen a man like...that," she whispered.

"Yes." Her reactions were too drastic to be faked. She was virginal all right, and her innocence excited him so much that he could hardly control the need to drag her under him and slake his thirst. But that would be wrong. "Christy."

She darted a glance at him, feeling threatened.

"It's all right to look," he said, his voice slow and tender.

She hesitated, but curiosity was too strong. Her eyes slid over him and back up again, her face scarlet. "You're so beautiful," she whispered, her voice hopelessly adoring.

The look on his face fascinated her. He frowned slightly, his eyes searching and curious. It wasn't a comment he'd expected from her.

Because she didn't understand the look, she was afraid she'd put her foot in her mouth again. She sat up, rearranging her disheveled clothing with hands that trembled.

He sat up, too, turning her to him. He didn't speak, but his eyes did. They were eloquent. He turned her across his legs, so that she could feel him intimately against her. When his mouth settled over hers again, she opened her own willingly, adoringly, and gave him complete access. His tongue thrust inside and she went limp in his arms.

"I can't take any more," he whispered, his voice deep and shaken as he lifted his head. "Cover me."

He held her up so that she could tug the sheet over his hips, concealing what he couldn't help.

He held her then until the faint tremor went out of his powerful body, until he could breathe normally again. "I want you," he said at her ear. "You'd better cut your trip short and go back to Florida."

She bit her lower lip. "Why?"

"You know why," he said with a bitter laugh. He tilted her face up to his mocking eyes. "My mother raised me to be a gentleman, but what I feel isn't so easily controlled. This time I mastered it. Another time, I might not. If you want to go to your marriage bed a virgin, you'd better get as far away from me as you can."

Chapter Six

Her mouth was swollen. She could barely get words through it at all. "I love you," she whispered miserably.

His jaw tautened. "No."

Her eyes lowered to his bare chest. "Are you…so certain?"

"Certain enough." He moved her over him and off the bed. "If you've never been intimate with anyone, it's easy to delude yourself into thinking physical attraction is love. I know. I did that once. But it doesn't last," he added quietly, his dark eyes cutting into hers. "This is nothing more than an interlude, and my fault. I shouldn't have touched you."

She looked down at him with anguish. He wanted sex and she wanted love. It was an impossible situation, and he was right. She should go home. She turned away toward the door.

"I'll get my things packed," she said.

"I didn't mean you have to leave today," he said tersely.

Good God, what was wrong with him, he thought furiously. He knew it was the best thing all around, for her to go quickly. But the thought of her leaving was like a knife in his chest.

"I should—"

"Not today!" he said curtly.

She turned around, her back against the door. She couldn't really see him clearly, but she could feel his rage. "You said it would be better," she reminded him.

He leaned back against his pillows, still taut with unsatisfied desire, and raked a hand through his thick black hair. "Probably it would, but you've got a responsibility to the group. I don't want to cost them a worker they need," he said, not looking at her. "I'll make sure this doesn't happen again. Despite what I said about your chastity, I'll send you home in your present condition. There won't be any more…interludes."

Could he know how much it hurt to think of never being held by him again, kissed by him? She sighed shakily.

"All right," she said. "Can I bring you anything?"

"No, thank you, honey," he said gently. "Go on. I'll be all right."

"I'll get back to work, then." She hesitated as she opened the door, not looking at him. "I'm glad you're not hurt," she said huskily. She closed the door behind her.

She didn't see Nate again until the next day. She'd been too embarrassed to go near him. It seemed to be that she went from shame to shame with him. First giving in so easily, then confessing that she loved him. She couldn't imagine what had possessed her to admit it, knowing that he felt nothing like that for her. But it had seemed so natural at the time.

George had been helping her sort pottery shards, in

between doing his own search of the area. She loved what she was learning about the *Hohokam*, despite the sting in her heart over Nate.

"One school of archaeologists believes that the *Hohokam* society thrived for over nine thousand years," George murmured as they studied the design on a large shard. "Imagine a society that stable, that unchanged."

"I can't," she said, brushing aside a stray wisp of hair. She was still going without makeup, without fixing her hair except into a soft bun, and without...

Well, what harm was there, she asked herself bitterly. She only had a few days left and she wasn't hurting anybody with this last little deceit. Besides, it was her own business.

She and George were still buried in their discoveries when it was time to go back to the ranch for supper. She piled into the equipment van beside George and thought about all that had happened since she'd come to Arizona, and wondered how she was going to live the rest of her life without Nate. She'd marry Harry and help get his kids through college, and then...and then what? The thought of being touched by Harry's pudgy hands made her sick.

She still looked nauseous when she got to the buffet line. Nate was standing in the doorway watching her, curious about the reason for that expression. He waited until she'd placed a meager portion on her plate and then he walked over and drew her by the arm to the table where his own coffee and food were waiting and seated her.

"What prompted that God-awful expression?" he asked, letting his dark eyes slip to the deep neckline of her sleeveless magenta blouse before they held hers.

"I was thinking about Harry's hands," she said without

considering her words, and then blushed as Nate's eyebrows went up to the neatly stitched cut on his forehead.

"Comparing them to mine?" he asked quietly.

She grimaced. "I wish you wouldn't," she murmured, glancing nervously around to see if anyone had heard. But the others were at the opposite end of the patio, talking shop as they sat together at three grouped tables.

He lifted a forkful of steak to his mouth, his smile faintly smug. "You'll pay a high price for that wedding ring if you don't enjoy having him touch you."

She stared down at her plate, hardly seeing anything on it. "I don't want to spend the rest of my life alone. I've had enough of that already. There will be compensations."

"Name one."

"I'll have someone to watch television with," she murmured dryly.

"Buy a dog. He'll have the added attraction of being someone to take on walks and buy presents for."

"I can take Harry on walks and buy presents for him," she said stubbornly.

His eyebrows arched. "Sure you can, honey, but the dog won't expect you to put his kids through college. Or can you tell me that Harry won't expect your help financially?"

"Harry and I agreed…" she began.

"Damn Harry," he said, his eyes kindling. His gaze fell to her soft mouth and lingered there. "I don't want supper. I want you."

"Don't," she moaned. She had to drag her eyes away from his. She forced herself to taste the steak. It was probably delicious, but she couldn't really savor it with him looking at her like that.

"I don't think I slept five minutes the whole night," he continued quietly. "What we did together haunted me."

"I don't want to have a love affair with you," she said, glaring at him.

"If you love me, why not?" he asked.

"Because sex is sordid without mutual feeling," she returned icily. "Don't you ever listen to the sermons when you go to church?"

He shrugged. "Not usually. You could go with us next Sunday and I'll try."

"I won't be here next Sunday," she said, and went white when she said it, because it was only then that she fully accepted that the group was leaving Saturday. Tears stung her eyes and made them suddenly bright, and her throat felt as if it had a pincushion in it.

His jaw tautened at the look on her face. "Don't look like that," he warned gruffly. "I'll come right over that table after you if you do, and to hell with gossip. I can't bear to watch you cry!"

She lowered her face and struggled for composure. "Why do you do this to me?" she wailed.

"Why do you do it to me?" he countered. "My God, do you realize I've been stuck out here in the sand for over three years without a woman? I've been celibate so long, I'm surprised that my body even remembered how to react when it had a half-naked woman against it!"

She looked up, shocked. "What?"

"I've been celibate for three years," he said, slowly as if she was too thick to understand words of more than one syllable. "You aren't the only one who had to do some renovating on yourself. I've never been much to look at, but I had money, so there was the occasional woman who gave her all

for a few luxuries in the past. But I hated being bedded for
my wallet, so I gave up on the fair sex. Then it dawned on me
that a man can work on his appearance if he wants to, so I lost
some weight and had my hair styled, got some new clothes
and…other things…and my life changed overnight. But
suddenly sex for its own sake wasn't enough. I seemed to lose
my taste for it. Until you came along," he added darkly, "and
complicated things."

"What did you look like before?" she asked, fascinated.

"Never mind. I'll show you a photo one day." His eyes
narrowed. "Saturday is too soon. You can stay."

"I can't, you know," she replied sadly. "Joyce Ann made
me promise to help her with her husband's banquet. She's a
hopeless cook, you see, and it's going to be a major occasion
for him. He's a junior partner in his business and two of the
big bosses are expected."

He smiled at her lazily. "Can you cook?"

"Yes. I'm not *cordon bleu*," she murmured, smiling back,
"but I used to win prizes at the fair for my pies and cakes."
She lowered her eyes. "I'm doing some French haute cuisine
for the banquet."

"You could come back, when it's over," he suggested.

She couldn't tell him that she wouldn't be able to afford
the plane fare again. Her pride wouldn't let her. She just shook
her head. "I have commitments."

"To Harry," he said icily.

She lifted her eyes. "Yes. To Harry. He may not be the
world's greatest lover, but he's kind and I'll have security."

"You'll have nothing," he said. "Nothing, except the
memory of what it was like to lie in my arms."

She bit her lip. "That's not fair."

"I can make it more than a harmless memory," he said, his voice deepening. "I could give you one long, endless night to carry back with you. We could go all the way."

Her eyes closed. She loved him, and he knew it, but it wasn't fair to taunt her like this. "I can't," she moaned.

"Look at me!"

The commanding tone brought her pained eyes up to meet his.

"I won't let you get pregnant," he said roughly. "And there's no danger of anything else with me, because I've never been promiscuous. I've been careful, in every way. I can give you something you'll never have with your stodgy prospective husband."

"I know that," she replied quietly, averting her eyes. "But I'd be cheating him out of something that's his due if he marries me. And you can sit there and harp on the new morality and my old-fashioned hang-ups until hell freezes over," she added when he started to speak, "but it's a matter of honor with me. If a man is willing to give me his name and be faithful to me, I owe him something in return. He has every right to expect fidelity in me."

He caught his breath. She was right. But he'd never thought of it like that. Fidelity. Honor. She was quoting words he'd said without understanding them. Now, suddenly, he did. She felt that she had to be faithful, even when there was no ring, when no vows had been spoken. A woman like that would never settle for any convenient bed partner after she was married, or indulge in casual affairs without seeing the harm in them. She'd marry one man, love one man, die faithful to one man. She'd have his children....

He stopped there. No, she wouldn't have Harry's children.

He didn't want any more. She'd die without having known the beauty of an infant in her arms, and it was so pointless. She was made to be a mother. He watched her ardently, trying to imagine how she'd look big with his own child inside her body, blooming in the fulfillment of motherhood. A scalding need surfaced in him, one he'd never realized he possessed. He wanted a family of his own. A wife. Sons. Daughters. He was thirty-seven years old and, except for his mother, totally alone. He had no one, really. But he wanted to have someone. He wanted Christy. His eyes narrowed. He hadn't really expected her to take him up on his offer of one wild night of love, although at the time, it had seemed perfectly sensible to offer it. Now he wasn't sure that he should have. She was a woman completely out of his experience. A woman with principles. He felt suddenly proud that a woman like that could love him.

"Fidelity," he repeated, watching her. "One man, one love. But if you don't love him, aren't you going to be cheating him, just the same?"

"I'll learn to love him," she said stubbornly.

"You said you loved me," he returned, and the words warmed him as he saw them hit the target.

She shifted restlessly in her chair. "You yourself said that that was just a cheap physical interlude," she returned, her voice wounded.

"I never said it was cheap," he returned. His eyes kindled. "That was the one thing it could never be, between you and me. My God, just the idea of letting a woman see me without my clothes was unthinkable only a week ago!"

She gasped. "You're not serious!"

"Why not?" he asked, his expression dark and formidable. "Do you think you're the only one with hang-ups? It was the most natural thing in the world to let you look at me, but I'd never have pulled that sheet away with any other woman."

Her eyes looked everywhere except at him, because the memory of what she'd seen was potent.

"And you needn't look so shocked," he replied. "You can't pretend that you've ever let your heartthrob back home look at you the way you let me."

She couldn't, she thought. She gazed at him across the table and her eyes adored the blurry line of his face. He was almost ugly, despite the self-improvement he'd mentioned, but it wasn't for his looks that he attracted women. There was a very definite masculinity in his personality, a take-charge attitude that was reassuring and comforting. Added to that was a tenderness she could feel in him, and a compassion that was deep and certain. He had qualities that appealed to everything womanly in her.

She picked at her meal halfheartedly. She had little appetite, and she was all too aware of time passing. She'd have to go home Saturday, back to her familiar world, but it was no longer an eagerly anticipated trip. She didn't know how she was going to survive leaving Nate.

"I've enjoyed being here," she said absently.

"It must have been a change for you," he replied.

"Sand is sand, they say," she murmured and smiled at him. "But there's such a difference between mine and yours."

"I suppose so."

She glanced up, her eyes lingering on the stitched red gash on his forehead, half obscured by his shock of dark hair. "How's your head?" she asked.

"Hard," he returned dryly. "I guess that's what saved me."

"I've never even been in a mine," she said.

"You haven't missed much." He leaned back with his coffee cup in his lean hand, watching her. "What does your Harry look like?" he asked.

He seemed to be pretty curious about Harry. Odd, when he didn't want a permanent relationship with her anyway. "He's a little taller than me," she replied. "Graying. He has a beer belly and he's sort of red-faced. He isn't handsome, but he's nice."

"I'm not handsome, and I'm not nice to boot."

She lifted her eyes to his face. "I wouldn't mind being trapped in a cave-in with you," she said simply. "Because I know you'd get us out one way or the other. Harry would sit down and give up. He isn't a fighter."

"You can do better than Harry," he said.

"Can I? I put on my best clothes and came out here with my changed image, and you thought I was a hooker," she reminded him.

"I did not," he returned, his eyes blazing. "I thought you were a gold digger."

"Thanks a lot."

"I didn't know you," he reminded her. He smiled slowly. "The real you came as quite a shock. I didn't plan on stopping that afternoon, out on the desert, you know," he added bluntly. "At that time, I had every intention of seducing you. Then I found out why you were so embarrassed when I looked at you."

"I'm sorry I gave you the wrong impression," she told him. "I wasn't trying to tease, even if it did seem that way."

"Yes, I've figured that out," he murmured, and there was a curious, knowing look on his face. "Are you going to be free tomorrow afternoon?"

The question thrilled her. She should have said "no" and played it safe, but she couldn't resist him. "Yes," she replied.

"I thought we might take in a movie in Tucson." He toyed with his cup. "There's a murder mystery that I've wanted to see."

He named it and she beamed. It was one she'd been looking forward to herself.

"I'd like that," she said.

He put down his cup, studying her long and hard. His slate eyes narrowed. "I'm too much a bachelor to offer you marriage," he said honestly. "And too much a gentleman to seduce you. I suppose we'll have to be friends, since that's all we have left."

"I wouldn't mind that," she lied.

"Neither would I. It gets lonely here." He turned the cup carefully on the table. "An occasional one-night stand doesn't do a thing for me anymore. I suppose I'm getting old." He looked up. "What we did together in my bed yesterday was a memory I'll treasure for the rest of my life."

"But we hardly did anything, really," she stammered.

"Didn't we?" He stood up, towering over her, his gaze long and steady on her uplifted face. She couldn't know how adoring her eyes were, how warm and caring and soft. They made him feel humble and guilty, all at the same time. He wished he was more of a gambler. If he had been, he'd have taken her away from Harry and married her out of hand and trusted to luck to keep them together. But it would be more of a risk than she realized. She was too unworldly, and her emotions were in a state of flux. He was afraid to take the chance that what she felt might only be infatuation.

"Sleep tight, honey," he said gently. He touched her hair as he passed her. "I'll see you tomorrow."

"Goodnight," she called after him.

She finished her meal and went into the recreation room

to watch the chess game with the group. She didn't want to be alone just yet with her thoughts, because they were too painful already.

The next afternoon, George left her alone while he helped Dr. Adamson with some measurements. She closed her eyes and felt the wind in her face, smelled the clean air with its faint scent of ancient pottery and desert vegetation. It was marvelous, the freedom she felt here, in this vast expanse of land. It seemed endless and wide open. Except for the total lack of trees in most places, it was very enticing. Of course, there were places in Florida where trees were scarce, too. But there was ocean and salt air all around, there.

It didn't get dark until late, so she wasn't aware of the passage of time. She sat down on a big boulder to brush sand off the design on a piece of pottery when two sounds impinged on her consciousness. One was the sound of an approaching Jeep, and she smiled to herself, because it had to be Nate coming after her. It touched her that he cared enough to do that, when she could have ridden in with the van.

But the other sound, the one that followed, was enough to chill her blood. She knew so well the noise that a rattlesnake makes. The Eastern diamondback is fairly common in south Georgia and northern Florida. The sound its rattle makes is unforgettable, like sizzling hot grease. This was the same sound, and she was aware that there was a Western diamond-back, a counterpart to the snakes she knew.

She knew better than to move. She sat very still, like a statue, and waited for Nate while she prayed that the snake wouldn't decided to sink its sharp fangs into her leg. Even if they got her to the antivenom in time, she would still be very sick until she recovered from the bite.

Nate would know what to do, thank God. She felt safer just knowing he was nearby. It would be all right.

"Christy?" She heard his deep voice calling her.

Did she dare answer, or would that venomous reptile be irritated by the vibrations of her voice and strike? If she didn't say something and Nate made much noise when he approached, it might happen anyway. She had nothing to lose, really.

She closed her eyes and bit her lip nervously. "Nate, there's a rattlesnake!" she called.

There was a rough curse and the sound of running footsteps. Barely a minute later, a lifetime later as she sat stiffly and prayed, the footsteps returned.

"Where is it?" he asked curtly.

"Somewhere near my left," she said, trying not to move a muscle. "I'm afraid to look."

"Sit still," he murmured, moving into her line of view. "Just sit still. You're doing fine. Managed to find a rattler, did you? I suppose you were camped on the only available shade. That rock you're sitting on juts out to keep the sun away. Good girl, you're doing fine, Christy."

She saw him move, his stride sure and deliberate. He was holding a rifle in the firing position, his eyes open and watchful as he moved slowly around in front of her. He looked like an old-time cowboy, she thought through her terror, with his Stetson pulled low over his eyes, wearing a Western-cut gray jacket and dark slacks. The snake was going to be sorry he'd tackled her now, she told herself. Nate was going to make a hatband out of the sneaky creature.

"Don't move, now. I see him."

She clamped her teeth together, steeling herself for the report when he fired. She knew without being told that he was a dead shot. It was in his confident aim, in the steely glitter of his eyes as he sighted, in the way he stood and shouldered the rifle.

He fired once and the rattling stopped. Christy jumped up and ran to him, throwing herself into his arms, shivering all over.

The lean arm that wasn't holding the rifle hauled her closer, bruising in its ferocity. "God Almighty, that was close!" he said harshly. "Didn't you look before you sat down? Not that it would have mattered, anyway, because what could you see?" he added, his voice cutting. "That's the last damned straw. You come with me."

He led her back to the Jeep, ignoring her questions, and put away the rifle. "She's all right," he told the others, who were gathered around, concerned. "Just a rattler, but he didn't strike her. I'll run her back to the ranch."

"I'm glad you're all right, Christy," George said with relief.

"So am I," she said, but she didn't get time to talk. Nate put her in the Jeep, got in beside her, and set new speed records for covering distance.

But he didn't stop at the ranch house. With his face hard and set, he screeched to a halt in front of her cabin and dragged her out of the Jeep to the door.

"Key," he said.

She fumbled it out of her pocket and gave it to him, puzzled by his attitude. He hadn't said one word to her all the way back, and he looked odd.

He unlocked the door, threw it open, and drew her inside. He pushed her gently down into a chair and began to go through drawers, oblivious to her shocked protestations. Minutes later, he found what he was looking for. He turned, with her huge-rimmed glasses in his hand and stuck them none too gently over her eyes.

"Now wear the damned things," he said shortly, glaring down at her with pure fury. "You little fool, you can't see five inches in front of you without those, can you? Did you think you could keep it up indefinitely? If you hadn't had good ears, you'd be in the hospital by now! Those rattlers are deadly."

"I know that…" she began, aghast at having been found out. Now that she could see him properly, she was a little afraid of him. He looked far more formidable with the lines stark and hard in his lean face. His eyes were much darker than she'd first thought, and there was a hardness, a ruthlessness about his face that intimidated her. If she'd been able to see him properly, like this, that first day, she'd never have had the nerve to even smile at him. He looked what he was—a hard-bitten desert man with no time for idiot tenderfeet.

"No wonder you fell over everything in your path," he muttered as he looked down at her. "If you don't want people to see you in specs, why don't you get contact lenses?"

"I tried," she confessed wearily, pushing her glasses up on her nose when they began to slip—as usual. "I had one eye infection after another, because I was too haphazard to keep them antiseptically clean, so they said I couldn't wear them. It's this or go blind." She looked at him mutinously. "I changed my whole image to come out here. The glasses spoiled it."

"What's wrong with glasses?" he asked carelessly. "I think you look better with them on. They make your eyes look bigger. Much sexier," he added with a grin.

Her green eyes widened. "Really?" she asked, forgetting her protests. He didn't think she looked awful!

"Really. Glasses aren't a cosmetic nuisance in your case, they're a necessity. Now keep them on. I don't want to lose you to a rattlesnake. I'm responsible for you."

That took a little of the pleasure out of his interest. She hesitated, her eyes sweeping over his hard features with quiet pain.

"You don't believe that bull about glasses making you less desirable?" he persisted.

She shrugged. "Men never noticed me before."

"I can understand that," he replied easily. "You're shy and introverted and you probably dressed to hide your body. Now you've put it on display and had your hair done and learned to use makeup. Glasses don't have anything to do with the qualities that make you desirable, Christy." He pulled her up against him and stood holding her, with his lean hands smoothing her bare arms in the white sleeveless top with the bulky yellow overblouse that kept her from burning in the sun. "Glasses or no, you're the sexiest woman I've ever known."

"You're only saying that to make me feel better...!"

He caught the words in his mouth and breathed them back into her own. She gave in immediately, too hungry for his touch to fight it now. Her arms reached under his and around him beneath his jacket and she pressed close, delighting in his instant arousal, in the sudden crush of his mouth against hers.

"That's it," he bit off. "Kiss me. Open your mouth. Yes. A little more. Don't hold back," he murmured roughly as he bent and lifted her. "Harder, baby. Do it harder!"

She felt him put her on the bed, felt his weight as he joined her on its narrow surface. His mouth was doing impossibly arousing things to hers, and his body was hard and urgent as it pushed her into the mattress. She felt the force of his heartbeat against her breasts, inhaled the faint scent of his cologne until she was drunk on it, drunk on him. His mouth was minty and hard and warm, and she never wanted to be free of it. She lifted closer into his embrace, feeling him shudder in response.

But even as she yielded, he lifted his head and muttered a curse.

"My God, it's impossible," he said huskily, sitting up as he struggled to catch his breath. His dark eyes swept over her prone body with possession and hunger, lingering on the thrust of her breasts under the low-cut white sleeveless top beneath her yellow overblouse. "We can't make love here. The damned bed's too flimsy for two people. It would fall through with us the first time we started moving back and forth on it."

She blushed scarlet. He smiled down at her with a knowing look in his dark eyes that got worse when her reaction was so transparent.

"Does it bother you to hear such blunt descriptions of love-making, Christy?" he asked, leaning over her to nip her lower lip gently with his teeth.

"Do you enjoy embarrassing me?" she demanded.

"Indeed I do. It's a rare treat to watch a woman blush in this day and time." He smoothed his hand blatantly over her breast, possessive demand in his touch while he gauged her helpless reaction. "You can't imagine how it feels, to watch you and know that what you're feeling is totally new."

"I guess it makes you feel conceited," she said defensively, embarrassed by his arrogance.

"No. It makes me feel proud." He let his eyes fall to where his hand was caressing her. "It means everything to me, being your first lover."

"But you aren't..."

His eyes went back up to hers. "I will be." He held her gaze for one long, endless moment before he slowly got to his feet and helped her up. He held her against him gently, his breath in her hair. "Did you hear me, Christy?" he whispered. "I'm going to be your first man. When it happens, it's going to be me."

"I'm marrying Harry," she whispered miserably.

"I don't think so." He drew her closer, sliding his hands to her hips and pulling them gently to his, letting her feel how aroused he was. "No, don't pull away from me," he said against her ear. "This reaction is yours alone. You don't have to be afraid of it. I told you I wouldn't seduce you and I meant it."

She relaxed finally and let him hold her. "I'm sorry about the snake," she murmured. "I know I should have worn my glasses. I could hardly see the boulders, although close up, my vision is very good."

He smoothed her hair gently in its disheveled bun. "You'll wear them from now on, do you hear me? I won't risk you twice. My God, when I saw that snake, I thought your number was up!"

"We both seem to be accident prone," she said on a forced laugh. "First you get caved in and then I get rattled at."

"We both need our heads examined." He drew back, glancing down at her. "Want to take a shower and change before we leave for Tucson?"

"Yes, if you don't mind."

"I don't mind." His thin lips tugged into a wicked smile. "I could wash your back."

She colored delicately. "No, you couldn't. I don't take showers with strange men."

"I let you look at me," he pointed out.

She glared at him. "Shame on you!"

He shrugged. "All right, be a prude. I'll have you out of your clothes one of these dark nights and under a sheet with me."

"I won't let you," she replied.

He tilted her chin up and brushed his mouth tenderly over hers. "Yes, you will. Have your bath. I'll be back in thirty minutes to get you." He searched her wide, soft eyes. "Harry can't make you pregnant. I can. If you loved him, that wouldn't matter. But if you don't love him, you might give that point some thought before you make up your mind."

She stiffened. "There's nothing to decide. He wants to marry me."

"No, I don't think that's a good idea," he said somberly. "He wouldn't enjoy raising my son as much as I would. Get your clothes changed, honey, I want to get an early start. We'll eat in town."

"Nate!" she said, exasperated.

But he left her there, trying to make sense of what he'd said. She finally gave up and got into the shower, still completely in the dark. He didn't want to marry her and here he was talking about his son. Sexist, she thought, how did he know it wouldn't be a daughter?

Which was beside the point, because she wasn't making any children with him when she was going to marry Harry!

Chapter Seven

Christy didn't have a large selection of dresses with her, and she'd already worn two of them. The third, and last, was a soft pink synthetic with a full skirt and button-up bodice, a large collar and cap sleeves. It suited her coloring beautifully, and emphasized her delicate complexion. She wore a scarf with complimenting colors and left her hair long. She glared at the glasses, but she put them back on. If Nate thought she looked all right, she supposed that was all that mattered.

She started to wear sandals, but mindful of the sand, she put on some white pumps instead.

Nate was waiting outside the cabin, still wearing his gray suit. He smiled at the picture she made in her dress. He couldn't imagine how she'd remained single so long, even if she hadn't prettied herself up. She had a sweet, caring nature and so many good traits that her looks were just a fringe benefit—not the reason he liked her.

"Nice," he pronounced, helping her into the car. "I hope you feel like Chinese food. I've got a yen for it tonight."

"I love it," she said. "Sweet and sour pork and egg rolls and hot mustard sauce! Yum!"

He chuckled. "My favorite, although I'm partial to pepper steak."

"Did I even thank you for rescuing me from the snake?" she asked as they drove along. "I was so shaken up, I don't remember."

"You aren't the only one. I was pretty shaken myself," he admitted. He glanced toward her. "Rattlers can kill, even in this day and time. And even if they don't, it's a painful experience. I took a bite in the leg when I was in my teens. They barely got me to the doctor in time, and I spent three days in the hospital. Damned thing still swells at the same time I was bitten every year," he chuckled. "They can't explain that, but it happens all the same."

"No wonder it bothered you that I almost got bitten," she murmured, thinking the memory would have resurfaced for him.

"It bothered me because I don't want anything to happen to you, Christy," he said.

"Because I'm a guest on your property," she nodded, understanding.

He scowled. "My God, do you believe that?" he asked angrily. "Hasn't it dawned on you yet that I was worried about *you*? It didn't have anything to do with your being a guest, or my old memories."

"No, it didn't occur to me," she said honestly. She smiled. "I'm not much to look at, even with my glad rags on…"

He muttered something violent under his breath and pulled off the road, into the privacy of the shade of a palo verde tree and stopped the car.

"I care about you." He said it slowly, looking straight into her eyes. He watched her blush. "That's right. I care. I don't want to, and it's interfering with my life and all my notions of freedom, but there it is. I just haven't quite decided what to do about it yet."

Her lips parted. She couldn't believe what she was hearing. Her heart was beating like a tom-tom deep in her chest, and the look in his eyes made her want to climb on top of the car and dance a jig.

"I'm glad. That you…like me, I mean," she added shyly. She looked down at his chest, noticing its heavy rise and fall. "I'm still sorry that I gave you the wrong impression at first."

"You didn't. I read what I wanted to read into the way you looked and acted. That was a defensive action." He sighed and traced her cheek with a lean, strong hand. "Oh, Christy, you're under my skin, girl. But there are so many reasons why I should let you go back to Jacksonville that I don't have a single argument for keeping you here," he said, and there was finality in his voice. That, and an expression that she couldn't quite understand in his eyes—a bleak look that puzzled her.

"I know that you don't want anything permanent," she said gently. "It's all right, Nate. I'm not asking for a single thing."

"That makes it harder to let go," he replied. He sighed softly. "Come here and kiss me, Christy."

He unfastened her seat belt and pulled her into his arms, kissing her slowly, and with a new tenderness. He wrapped her up in his lean arms, and his mouth asked things of her that it hadn't before. It asked for comfort, for reassurance. It asked for love.

She slid her arms around his neck and gave him back the soft, slow kiss without a thought of withdrawal. Even when his hands found her breasts and cradled them with quiet possession, she didn't protest. She belonged to him. He had every right to touch her.

His head lifted. His arm tightened around her while his free hand loosened the buttons of her bodice and slid inside. He watched her face while he touched her. "Anything I want?" he whispered softly.

"Yes," she confessed.

He bent and brushed his mouth lazily over hers. She felt the cool air wash over her, because the bodice had been pulled away and so had her bra. Her breasts, hard-tipped and swollen, lay open to his warm gaze in the dim light of the setting sun.

He looked down at her body with reverence, his hand going slowly to trace the exquisite curve of one firm breast. "It's never been like this with a woman," he said huskily. "There was never time...like this." He tried to put it into words. His dark gray eyes slid up to hers. "There was always urgency and haste, even when I thought my emotions were involved. There wasn't this tenderness, this need to cherish, to give."

Her lips parted. He didn't seem to understand what he was describing, but she did. It was what she felt for him. It was love. Perhaps he hadn't realized it just yet. She smiled gently, her eyes so soft and caring that she heard his breath jerk when he looked into them.

"Christy, you're exquisite," he breathed. His eyes moved back down to the beauty his hand was exploring. His fingers trembled on her body. "Exquisite, and I want you so badly, honey…!"

She touched her lips to his throat, feeling him quiver at the contact. He caught his breath and bent to take her mouth under his. He groaned, his hand suddenly warm and insistent as he cupped her.

"Nate," she whispered ardently.

She arched her back, pulling his mouth down to her breasts. She cried out at the pleasure his hungry touch gave her, moaning as the pressure increased and his hands contracted on her waist.

He said something violent under his breath and buried his face in her warm throat. His arms enveloped her roughly and he rocked her in the heady silence of the car, his arms faintly tremulous with the force of his passionate need. God, she was sweet to love! But she was grass green and in the throes of her first physical intimacy, and he didn't trust her feelings enough to take a chance on them, despite the fact that he couldn't bear the thought of letting her leave him.

Christy smoothed his dark hair, guilty that she'd let things go this far again when she hadn't meant to. It was hurting him to hold back.

"I'm sorry," she whispered at his ear. "I seem to keep saying that. I don't want to hurt you."

He actually laughed, deep in his throat. "You can't imagine what a sweet hurt this is, for a man," he whispered. "A kind of slow, throbbing ache laced with vicious pleasure."

"I feel that way, too," she confessed shakily. Her arms contracted and she was tempted beyond imagination. "Nate, you said that you could…keep me from getting pregnant," she blurted.

He stiffened. She wanted him. God, he wanted her, but not like this. Not in a parked car, in desperation. No. He wanted her honorably, or not at all, and his own scruples stopped him.

His mouth brushed her ear. "No." He kissed her closed eyes, feeling her puzzlement. "I can't."

"But…"

"Don't tempt me," he breathed. "Don't ask me to tarnish something this beautiful by reducing it to raw sex."

Her breath stopped in her throat. So he did feel something! He had to, or why would he have refused when she could feel his need?

His head lifted, and her eyes were full of awed adoration.

"And that's the first time I've backed away from satisfaction," he said flatly. His eyes searched hers. "There isn't another woman on earth I wouldn't take right here, sitting up if I had to. But it's different with you, Christy. So different."

She smiled, and her face radiated love. "Yes."

He smoothed back her hair and his eyes involuntarily dropped to the open bodice of her dress. "No white lines," he whispered, smiling at her shyness.

"It's too hot to sunbathe," she murmured. "And I haven't been to the beach this year."

"Do you sunbathe topless?" he asked.

She laughed self-consciously. "No. I'm too inhibited."

"I'm glad. I don't like to think of other men seeing you this way," he said slowly. He bent and put his lips reverently to her breasts before he rearranged her clothing to cover her.

When she'd brushed her hair with the small brush in her purse, and restored her lipstick, she had a radiance that made her beautiful enough to stop Nate's breath in his throat.

"I'm going to have to let you go home, Christy," he said through his teeth. "You know that."

She looked at him. "Yes. I know." He could have loved her, she was sure of that, but it was commitment that stopped him dead. She could understand it, too. He was thirty-seven. He'd been a bachelor too long, and now the thought of giving up his freedom was impossible. She didn't know how she was going to manage to go on living without him, but there was no question of her staying here and they both knew it. Like an amputation, it would be better to get it over with as quickly as possible.

He looked at her long and hard, with a dark, unfathomable expression in his eyes. "We'd better get going," he said, turning away finally to start the car again.

Christy fastened her seat belt with steady fingers. She could take it, she told herself. And at least she'd have beautiful memories of this trip, and dreams of how it might have ended. Perhaps they'd sustain her through the years ahead.

The one thing she was certain of now was that she couldn't possibly marry Harry. Nate had been right about that. It would be cheating him as well as herself, feeling the way she did about Nate. But she needn't go into that, she thought, glancing at Nate. Let him think she'd be married and settled and not dying of love for him. She didn't want him to be concerned for her happiness, or guilty because she wanted more than he could give. It was better if he thought her marriage plans were final.

They ate, but without any real enthusiasm, and Nate kept the conversation on a strictly impersonal level. Inside, he was on fire. He wanted to tell her she couldn't go home and to hell with Harry, that he'd take care of her, that he'd love her. But she had to have time to make sure that what she felt was going to last, that it wasn't just the adventure and different environment blinding her to reality. He owed her that. He owed himself that, he added. Marriage was forever to him. He wasn't going to risk it on a brief infatuation. She had to be sure.

Nate took Christy back to her cabin and kissed her good night, but gently and without lingering. And for the rest of the week, he was pleasant and polite and mostly too busy to spend any time with her. Christy understood that he was making the parting easier for her, so she didn't complain. She stuck with George and did her best to blot out the memory of Nate's lips and arms while the last few hours of her holiday ticked away with relentless speed.

Saturday came before she was ready. She was packed and dressed for travel in her jeans and a loose white sweatshirt and sneakers, because the plane was air-conditioned and frankly cold with her arms uncovered. She joined the others at the front of the house, where the van was waiting to take them to the airport.

Nate came out to say goodbye, saving Christy for last. She looked at him with pain and longing, wishing that she could hide her despair well enough to make him think she didn't mind going. She didn't want him to feel sorry for her now, even though she'd hoped right up until the last minute that he'd change his mind, that he'd confess undying love and propose marriage. But that didn't happen, and she knew she shouldn't have expected it. He wanted her, but he'd get over that. Desire and a little tenderness weren't enough to build a future on, although she'd have tried it if he'd been willing. She loved him so much that she had no pride at all.

He drew her to one side, his eyes lancing over her face like a paintbrush, memorizing every soft line of it. He was hurting, but he didn't dare show it. She had to be free.

"Take care of yourself," he said quietly.

"You, too." She bit back tears and laughed self-consciously. "I'm sorry. I promised myself I wouldn't do this."

He cupped her faced in his lean hands and his thumbs brushed away the tears. His dark eyes were soft with concern and something deeper that she was too blurry to see. She hadn't put on her glasses this morning, because she didn't want to see too clearly.

"Don't fall down the steps. You should have your glasses on," he said gently.

That concern in his deep voice almost brought the tears back. "I won't fall." She reached up and brushed his lean cheek with her lips. "Goodbye, Nate. Thanks for a lovely holiday. I'll never forget it. Or you."

He didn't return the caress or the sentiment. He looked down at her with his heart like lead in his chest, feeling empty and alone already.

His hands fell away from her face. "You'd better get on board," he nodded toward the van.

Her lips trembled into a smile. "Yes, I had." She'd hoped that he might at least kiss her goodbye, but with all these other people around, he probably felt it would be too public a demonstration. He was letting her go, wasn't he? "Well, goodbye," she faltered. She smiled again and, dragging her eyes away from him, she shouldered her pocketbook and climbed into the van.

Nate didn't wait to see it leave. He climbed into his car and headed for work without looking back. He couldn't have borne seeing the van drive away, taking Christy out of his life.

Christy put on the one pair of prescription dark glasses she had, wondering why she hadn't thought to wear them sooner. That way her fellow travelers couldn't see the tears.

George, bless him, knew what was wrong. He sat beside her, holding her hand unobtrusively.

"I'd like to keep in touch with you," he said. "We could write each other at Christmas, at least."

"That would be nice," she said, and meant it.

He smiled. "Fine. I'll write down my address for you."

She settled back into her seat. Only a few hours more and she'd be home in her own apartment. Then she could have a good cry and try to put the past three weeks out of her mind. She had a few souvenirs that she was going to put in a drawer until she could stand to look at them and remember. Meanwhile, it was going to be trouble enough just to walk around normally.

In the weeks that followed, she wondered how she survived the black depression that settled over her. Joyce Ann was openly concerned, and more so since Christy had said a definite and final "no" to Harry.

"It's the Arizona caveman, isn't it?" the older woman demanded, pushing back her gray-streaked blond hair with an angry hand as they sat in Joyce Ann's immaculate living room drinking coffee. "You haven't been the same since you came back. Honestly, Christy, it's been two months, and you walk around like a zombie! You won't go anywhere, you just sit at home and moon!"

Christy had lost weight. She knew she looked bad, but she had no interest in life anymore. Odd, that, when she'd loved the simplest things before. Things like sitting on the beach, listening to the gulls while the salt breeze whipped through her hair and the whitecaps foamed onto the damp sand. Things like going to art galleries to browse and sitting in small cafes drinking coffee and watching people. But she'd changed since her trip to Arizona. She wasn't the same woman who'd gone on an archaeological expedition looking for lost civilizations.

"Pre-planning starts the end of the month," she told Joyce Ann, barely listening to what her sister was saying. "School will be good for me."

"I hope so. Darling, you're positively skeletal, and you don't even bother to dress up and fix up anymore. There are the most terrible dark shadows under your eyes." She shook her head. "Christy, I'm worried about you."

"I'll get over him," Christy assured her. "Really, I will."

Joyce Ann sighed, frowning. "I've never had the courage to ask, but is there any chance, well, that you might be pregnant?"

Christy smiled. "No. That would make the Guinness Book of World Records for sure. He was a perfect gentleman, even when he didn't want to be."

That made it all worse somehow, Joyce Ann thought. Why would a man with sex on his mind bother to hold back? On the other hand, why would a man in love be willing to let her go?

"Oh, Christy. What can I say?" she asked helplessly.

"Just that you love me," Christy replied, and hugged the older woman tight.

Joyce Ann sighed as she returned the embrace. Somehow it seemed unfair that Christy should finally find a man to love and lose him in so short a time. But that happened sometimes. She could only hope that Christy would recover in time.

It was almost dark and Joyce Ann's husband was due home

when Christy left for her own apartment. She got in her compact car and drove home without paying any attention at all to her surroundings. If she had been, she might have noticed the vehicle sitting across the road from where she lived, and the man watching her from the driver's seat.

But, oblivious, she parked the car, got out, and went to unlock the door. As she turned on the light inside, she heard footsteps behind her and turned.

Her heart stopped beating; at least, that was how it felt. Her heart had fed on memories for weeks. She hadn't taken a camera to Arizona, due to an oversight in packing, so she hadn't even a photograph of him to keep. But here he was, in the flesh, looking every bit as terrible as she did.

He came closer, and she felt her jaw drop. This wasn't the Nate she remembered. He was wearing glasses with silver rims, sporting tan slacks with a white shirt and a conservative gray and tan sports coat. He wasn't wearing a hat or boots, and his hair was unruly and a little long.

"Nate?" she asked hesitantly.

He was doing some staring of his own. She had her hair in a bun, no makeup on. She was wearing a green dress that did nothing for her, and with her glasses on, she could see him very clearly. He looked thinner, too, and there were dark circles under his eyes that matched those under her own.

"It's me," he said, pausing to tower over her in the doorway, with night falling rapidly over his shoulder. "The real me," he added with a faint smile. "This is the way I looked before you saw me."

Her eyes adored him. "I like you this way," she said softly. "This way, the other way, any way!" Her voice wobbled and tears burst from her eyes.

"Come here!" he groaned, reaching for her.

His arms enfolded her even as his hard, hungry mouth found her own. He held her and kissed her with all the anguish of two months of loneliness, glorying in her headlong response, in the softness of her body in his arms, the sweetness of her open mouth accepting the hard thrust of his tongue. She trembled, and he felt that, and smiled against her lips.

"What a welcome," he breathed against her smiling mouth. "You'll make me conceited."

"You know how I feel. I made no secret of it," she said huskily, her eyes telling him everything.

"And I had to," he said, his eyes dark and possessive. "I had to keep my feelings to myself until I was sure of yours. My God, you look terrible! Almost as bad as I do. Has it been hard?"

"Impossible," she confessed. Her eyes adored him. "I thought I was going to wither and die."

"Same here." He held her close, rocking her, his lips in her hair. "I suppose your neighbors will think you're harboring a lover," he mused, glancing around at the other buildings.

"I am," she whispered. "Because that's what you're going to be."

"Eventually," he agreed, lifting his head to smile down at her. "I want you like hell, but we're going to do this the right way around. First we get married."

"Oh, Nate!" she said, feeling heaven in her grasp.

"I hope that idea appeals to you as much as it appeals to me," he said, his voice deeper, softer as he looked down into her eyes. "I don't want to live if I can't have you."

"Neither do I." She reached up, touching his lean cheek, adoring him. "Why did you let me go?" she asked in anguish.

"I had to, honey," he said gently. "I was your first real

beau. You were so vulnerable, especially in a physical sense. I didn't want to take advantage of you. You had to have time to be sure that you loved me."

"What do you think?" she murmured. "Do I?"

He chuckled at her saucy scrutiny. "Yes, I think so," he said, his eyes kindling. "I think so, Miss Haley."

"Have you had anything to eat?"

His eyebrows arched. "No. Can you find us some bread and mayonnaise and sandwich meat, or do you want to go out and eat?"

"I've got quiche in the refrigerator and the makings of a delicious fruit salad. If you'd like that," she added hesitantly.

"Oh, I don't believe that bit about real men not eating quiche," he said easily, and grinned. "It's one of my favorite dishes."

"Mine, too." She sighed. "My sister will be surprised."

"Joyce Ann?" He laughed out loud, ushering her into her apartment and closing the door behind them. "No, I'm afraid the surprise is yours."

She put down her purse and turned to him. "What do you mean?"

"Who do you think called me long distance to ask why the hell I was killing her baby sister?"

"Joyce Ann didn't!" she burst out. "She couldn't!"

"She did," he interrupted. "Thank God she did, I was at the end of my rope. Another week and I'd have been sitting on your doorstep anyway. But it was nice to have some advance notice of how you were taking my absence." The humor went out of his lean, dark face. "I want you to love me," he said huskily. "I've never wanted anything so much. So will you please tell me you don't believe in long engagements, even if you do?"

She slid into his arms and lifted her mouth to his. "I think three days *is* a long engagement. Can I go home with you?"

"Is that what you want?" he asked, frowning. "Arizona is pretty different from what you're used to…"

"I love Arizona," she said softly. "I love the land and the people and the history of it. Most of all, I love it because you do. I can teach anywhere, Nate. I have a feeling teachers are pretty important in your neck of the woods. I'll be doing work that will have meaning, important work."

"In that case, yes, you can come home with me. Do you want to be married here?"

"Joyce Ann would never get over it if we didn't," she murmured. "But what about your mother?"

"She adores you. She'll look forward to having you around. But I thought we might build a house of our own," he began.

"Who's going to help your mother and Nita if we desert them?" she asked reasonably. "Do be sensible. I don't have a mother. Yours is super. I don't want a house of my own."

He shook his head, adoring her with his eyes. "Whatever you want, honey," he said quietly. His face hardened with passion. "I love you," he whispered, bending toward her.

Her lips met his and she closed her eyes, reaching up to him. He lifted her and carried her to the nearest armchair, sitting down with her in his lap. The kiss deepened and lengthened, and Christy thought she'd never been so happy in all her life.

By the time he finally lifted his demanding mouth, she was trembling and more than a little bare flesh was on view. He smiled at her with dark appreciation and laughed at her shyness.

"Three days," he said. "I'll get a motel room and we'll spend every available hour together. Then, on the third night, I expect to get as little sleep as possible."

She laughed and pressed her face against his bare chest, enjoying the abrasive sensuality of the rough hair that covered it. "So do I," she said. "I hope I won't disappoint you too much."

"Well, let me put it this way," he said, tilting her eyes up to his amused ones. "Having a greenhorn along on a cattle drive would be hard on the nerves. But having a pretty greenhorn in bed..." He brushed his mouth lovingly over hers. "Now that, Miss Haley, is a prospect that I look forward to with pure delight. Enough said?"

She sighed and traced his hard mouth with a slow forefinger. "Enough said," she whispered.

They were married exactly three days later, with Joyce Ann and her husband for witnesses. Christy wore a white satin dress with a short lace veil, and as Nate lifted the veil to kiss her for the first time as her husband, the look in his eyes brought tears to her eyes. Love was there, and tenderness, and desire, all three as radiant as the sun outside the small church. Christy lifted her lips to his, and gave him her heart.

* * * * *

LOOK OUT...

...for this month's special product offer.
It can be found in the envelope
containing your invoice.

**Special offers are exclusively for
Mills & Boon® Book Club members.**

You will benefit from:

- Free books & discounts
- Free gifts
- Free delivery to your door
- No purchase obligation – 14 day trial
- Free prize draws

THE LIST IS ENDLESS!!

*So what are you waiting for —
take a look* **NOW!**